Straw into Gold

by

Gary D. Schmidt

Clarion Books New York

Clarion Books
a Houghton Mifflin Company imprint
215 Park Avenue South, New York, NY 10003
Copyright © 2001 by Gary D. Schmidt

The text was set in 12-point Italian Old Style.

www.houghtonmifflinbooks.com

Printed in USA.

Library of Congress Cataloging-in-Publication Data

Schmidt, Gary D.
Straw into gold / by Gary D. Schmidt.
p. cm.
Summary: Pursued by greedy villains, two boys on a quest to save innocent
lives meet the banished queen whose son was stolen by Rumpelstiltskin eleven
years earlier, and she provides much more than the answer they seek.
ISBN 0-618-05601-7
[1. Fairy tales. 2. Greed—Fiction.] I. Title.
PZ8.S2845 St 2001   [Fic]—dc21   00-060340

QUM   10 9 8 7 6 5

For Anne,
who knows what fills a hand fuller
than a skein of gold

The Miller's Daughter

Once when the world was younger and the times ever so much older, there lived a miller who ground coarse flour, left stone chips in his meal, and stole as much wheat as he could take without his customers knowing for certain that they had been robbed. His mill hunched ramshackle beside a dwindling river, its wheel lumbering in a circle like a blind beast at a tether. When the lumbering wheel stopped, the miller would slouch to his gray, sloping cottage and sit silent at the meals his wife and daughter set, wishing for what he did not know. He no longer attended Mass, and when the priest came to chide him, he spat on the floor. He abandoned the markets in Wolverham and grew surly with those few customers who still brought their wheat to him. Finally they too left him alone, ramshackle himself beside silent millstones.

One twilight the king and his hunters rode by the mill just as the miller was coming out. The miller looked at the embroidered clothes of the hunters, their beringed fingers, their golden spurs, the silver studs on their dogs' collars, and suddenly he could not bear to have them ride by without noticing him.

"Your Majesty," the miller shouted. But when the king stopped, the miller did not know what to say.

Snickers from the huntsmen, and the king took up his reins again. "Majesty," called the miller desperately, "I have a daughter, the most beautiful in all your land, if it please you."

The king pulled away, but the miller dashed in front of the horse and grabbed at the reins. "Her beauty is such that everything she touches becomes as beautiful as she. Even straw slips from her spinning wheel into golden thread."

The setting sun silhouetted the king, so the miller could not see the greed that sprang into his face. "Golden thread?" he repeated.

"The finest of gold," the miller insisted, "skeins of it, gleaming brighter than the sun!"

"Bring her to Wolverham tomorrow, and we shall see if what you say is true. Should she indeed be able to spin straw into gold, she will be rewarded richly. And you along with her. If not, you have lost your daughter her life." The miller let go of the reins and watched the king's company ride away laughing. Then he turned to the river and wished that it were deeper and swifter.

When the miller told the tale to his wife and daughter that night, tears scoured his cheeks, but his daughter held him close. "We shall see what comes with the day," she said. But the new day brought only gray and dismal clouds shrouding the road to Wolverham, and gray and dismal hearts held tight in the miller and his daughter. When finally stood before the king, they both trembled.

The miller's daughter was indeed as beautiful as the miller had said, and because she hid her trembling, the king saw her standing like a noble and stately princess. He dismissed the miller with a wave of his hand and welcomed the daughter to his castle. He sent for attendants to dress her for the revels that would be celebrated that night in her honor, and when she was brought back to him in the early evening, he was dazzled by the play of firelight upon her face.

But something was missing.

A clap and a whisper to an attendant, who disappeared at a run. He soon reappeared behind the miller's daughter, holding an open wooden chest.

"Lady, you are bidden to wear these." Inside, a wrought golden ring and a square-linked golden chain glowed against the velvet. She held her hand up, and the servant slipped the ring on. Then he took the chain and fastened it behind her neck, the king watching all the while.

Late that night, the king almost regretted bringing her to the room of straw to do what no one could do. But he had said what he had said, and now he pointed to the spinning wheel and the surrounding hillocks of straw. "If you cannot spin this straw into gold, you will surely die." He lay wakeful that night, knowing that he would doom her to execution the next morning.

The miller's daughter was also awake, pacing around the spinning wheel, weeping. When the locked door opened suddenly, she was startled to think that morning had come so quickly. But it had not, and it was not the king coming to seize her. Instead, a little man entered and bowed.

"Why is Mistress Miller crying?" he asked politely.

"This straw must be spun into golden thread by morning."

"And is that all? Simply done. But what does she have that will pay for the spinning?"

She removed the golden chain easily from her neck and handed it to the little man.

"Done," he said, and sat at the spinning wheel, filling spindle after spindle with skeins of golden thread.

In the morning the king was astonished at what he saw, and if love of the miller's daughter grew in his heart, it warred with the greed that grew even faster. He took her to a second room, piled higher with straw, and demanded that it too be spun into gold by morning. As before, the little man appeared while she lay weeping, and when she handed him the ring from her finger, he sat at the wheel, filling spindle after spindle with skeins of golden thread.

The next morning the king drew open the door eagerly, and he was not disappointed at what he saw. And if his love grew stronger, his greed grew even wilder, and he took the miller's daughter to a third room, filled almost to the ceiling with straw bundled from the barns of every farmer near Wolverham. He left her with the same warning: She must spin this straw into gold, or she would die. But if she succeeded, he promised, she would become his wife. At this she hid her face. For joy, the king thought.

When the little man appeared the third time, he again demanded that the miller's daughter give him something before he sat down to spin.

"I have nothing left to give," she said.

"Then Mistress Miller must promise to deliver her first child to me."

She felt a hand grip her heart, and her tears blurred the little man.

"Promise," he insisted. "Mistress Miller must promise, or the king will find only straw when he opens the door."

"I cannot promise such a thing," she said quietly.

"It is peril I speak of. Peril. Mistress Miller must yield the child."

"Whose peril?"

"She must yield the child," he repeated.

So she promised, and when the king found a room of golden skeins upon opening the door, he swept them into his treasury and the miller's daughter into his throne room.

A year later the miller's daughter, now the queen, birthed a son, and the hand that still held her heart gripped even more fiercely. She hid her terrible promise deep within her, but in the summer evenings as she nursed the boy at her breast, and on clear autumn mornings when he stretched his fingers to the golden leaves, and during winter nights when she tucked him warmly beneath heavy robes, she felt the grip of the hand.

One day, when the child's eyes were no longer their infant blue, what she feared came. As she sat in her bedchamber, rocking her sleeping boy, the door fell back and the little man strode in, his arms outstretched to take the child. "Now Mistress Miller must give me what she promised."

She stood up, clutching the baby, unable to speak.

"None of this. None of this," said the little man, coming closer. "What's spun is spun. The child is mine, as Mistress Miller promised. Yield the child."

"Anything," the miller's daughter said, shaking her head, "anything of mine is yours. Anything but this child."

"She has nothing but this child to give."

The miller's daughter pled and wept until the little man at last relented. "But for three days only, no more."

"Is that all that I may hope for?"

The little man thought for a moment, his eyes strangely sorrowful. "Each day," he said slowly, "she may guess three names while I hold the child. If by the third day she has guessed my name, she shall keep him. If not, she shall give him to me."

"And if the king should place guards at the gates of Wolverham, and by the castle, and by my own door?"

"Mistress Miller knows," whispered the little man, "whether the king will stretch his hand out to protect her. She knows better than I."

Silence, terrible and long, until the miller's daughter murmured, "I agree," and the little man was gone.

In the morning he appeared, holding out hands with fingers as long as spindles. The miller's daughter had prepared three strange and unusual names, but when she saw her baby in the little man's hands, drawn close to his chest and wailing, wailing, wailing for all the world, she blurted out, "Matthew, Mark, Luke," and grabbed the child back. The little man left silently.

On the second day the miller's daughter called the names even before he took the child from her arms, but the little man shook his head. "Promises by Mistress Miller are not so easily broken. She may try the names while I hold the baby," and he took her son from her arms.

"Plotinus, Justinius, Boethius," she said, snatching the child back. Once again the little man left silently.

On the third day the little man appeared with a basket, lined with a blanket woven through with golden thread. The eyes of the miller's daughter were wide and stricken, but the child's were closed in silent sleep. Wordlessly the little man took the baby, wrapped him in the blanket, and placed him in the basket.

"Basil," said the miller's daughter hopelessly.

The little man picked up the basket.

"Jerome."

He walked to the doorway and paused there, looking back. "One more guess for Mistress Miller." But she could not speak, so closed was her throat. When he left and the door shut behind him, the hand gripped her heart so terribly that she fell into a heap.

chapter one

I had waited for this day for as long as I could remember.

And now, lying under a down quilt, I folded my arms behind my head and savored the day's bright coming. Outside the window, across dark woods and blue hills, fingers of sunlight reached over the edge of the world. They reached farther and farther as the sun shouldered up behind them, the light whitening the hills, the evergreens, the very air, until finally it spread into my own room and played on the quilt.

I had waited for this day.

A rap at my door. "Up, up, up!" My da. Morning after morning our life had a sameness to it, and even if today was the day when I would finally go to Wolverham, when I would see the market and the castle and the townspeople, when the king himself would process to celebrate a great victory, there were still the morning chores. And today the Dapple and the Gray would need special care. After the feeding and mucking out, they would have to be curried, combed, and saddled. It was a chore I enjoyed almost as much as they did, but today it meant a longer time before we could leave.

"I'm up! I'm up!"

The door creaked itself open and Da peered in. "Up is dressed. Up is walking across the yard with a bucket in each hand. Up is milking. Up is not lying under a quilt with arms back of his head."

"Fuss bucket," I hollered.

"He is a slugabed." Da shook his head, the tip of his beard wagging just over his toes. Then he padded away down the hall, hooting like a comic owl. The door quietly latched behind him.

Some things about this morning were the same.

The casement windows cut the sunlight into diamond streaks that patterned the floor, but when my feet hit the stone, the chill in them shivered me. I threw three splints on the graying embers and blew them to a blaze. When my face and hands were warmed, I lifted my shirt and turned my back to the fire. My breath blew into the room like a cloud.

Wolverham. I'd never seen the city, but on the clearest of days, when the sky was bluer than blue and the clouds whiter than white, I could climb the thatch of our roof and just barely see the banners braving the castle turrets. I imagined them rollicking in the breeze and thought what a fine place it must be, where houses lay stone against stone, one after another, up to the castle itself. For someone who had never been past the clearing around our home, such a thing would have been impossible to imagine without the pictures that Da had conjured in the air many a late evening.

Down in the kitchen the buckets of water were just hovering beside the cooking pot. At Da's wave they tipped their water in and then stacked themselves by the side door, the top one lying slanted for a moment until Da's frown eased it right. He took a pipe from his vest pocket and tapped it with his thumbnail until the smoke started to rise.

"It's the day," I said. "Da, it's the day."

"It is, it is," he said. "Though he will have a cold ride, no doubt. Maybe snow by noon, or worse." He took a long pull from the pipe, then puffed out a billowed cloud, and another, and another, until it seemed about to blizzard in the kitchen.

"It's the brightest day we've had all winter long."

Da waved his arms in the air and the clouds shredded into nothing. "But then he'll be disappointed by the town, thinking it is all as grand as can be and finding it is nothing like."

"It will be grand enough for someone who has never seen it."

"And then the king will have a cold in his nose and be unable to march in the procession."

"He'll process. He has a victory to celebrate. There will be trumpets, and horsemen, and Lord Beryn's Guard, and the king himself."

At this, Da's face darkened.

"Well," he said, "he'll have to hope it will be a brave new day after all. Now, if he tends to the milking and to the Dapple and the Gray, breakfast will be ready when he gets back in. And the dinner to take. And he should tend the one sore on the Dapple's foreleg. He'll need that balm." He turned back to the fire and twisted his palm to ignite the kindling. The logs eased close in to the flames.

The clearing was bright with light, as it always was, every morning. The air was cold enough to startle me to wakefulness, and the larks—the larks who sang all year round—they were enough to startle my soul. Their songs trilled the air. But though I stood each morning to fill myself with the delight of it all, I had lately begun to notice not so much the open clearing as the trees that bounded it.

It had begun to seem a very small clearing. And the world beyond it to be very large.

I had begun to wonder how large the world was.

I had begun to wonder how large I was.

In the barn I stripped the milk faster than it pleased the Milcher, then set the bucket outside in the cold while I tended to the horses. They knew the world was different this day, and I could hardly comb them for their nuzzling. And the Dapple would not stand still for me to spread the balm until I poured a double handful of grain into his trough.

Wolverham. For days I had thought of nothing else. The lessons that Da taught—the geography of lands yet to be discovered, the mathematics of travel through the air, the texts of books by authors still waiting to be born—they flew past me like night phantoms. To see a king, *the* king— what could be grander? Slogging the milk bucket across the clearing, I wished the horizon would hold the sun in the curve of its scythe to keep the day from racing on too quickly. Once more I looked at the boundary trees.

Da had breakfast ready: thickened oatmeal spread with cinnamon and honey, and juice from a yellow fruit that never grew in this kingdom. I set the bucket down, and as the pitcher filled itself from it, I fetched the brown bread that waited patiently in the brick oven.

"Perhaps Tousle will be disappointed in the king if he is not all he expects? After all, he is a man like other men."

"But a king, Da. A king. With armies at his every command, and courtiers bowing beneath his scepter, and kingdoms quaking at his name." I stood on the bench and waved my arms. "Conquer this realm. Build that castle. Do as I command."

"And what is his lordship's command?" asked Da, bowing low.

"A vision of the king, my servant."

And suddenly in the air there was the king riding in procession, his hand on his hip, his armor brighter than armor could ever be. He plucked his golden sword from its golden scabbard and swung it in circles over his head, cutting through the air. He looked as if he could stride across the world and conquer the globe. There were no trees bounding his clearing.

"And the queen," I called out. "Your lord commands a vision of the queen."

"And his lordship's commands are to be obeyed," answered Da, and bowed again.

The king passed out of the air, and behind him came a lady who seemed to move in quietness. She wore a thin diadem whose silver circle faded in and out of the gray streaks that marked her brown hair tucked beneath. She held the reins loosely and rode with the roll of one who knew how. If she had looked up, she might have shown eyes that were as knowing as her hands. If she had spoken, her soft voice would have stilled the heart. But she did neither.

"Da," I said.

"The queen."

"But she looks . . ."

"Like someone who has lost something," he finished.

Then the queen rode out of the edge of the procession into a blurred mist and was gone.

And suddenly I was quiet. I felt something stirring deep down that had never stirred before. It was as mysterious as a dream where I was all alone, searching for something I could not name, could not even imagine, but would know once I found. "Bring her back," I asked, "just for a moment."

"Is Lord Tousle commanding?"

"Tousle is asking."

"Well, majesty is never diminished by grace. But he will see her soon enough. Now Lord Da commands that Tousle come off the bench and eat his breakfast. The oatmeal has cooled, and here is the brown bread asking to go back to the brick oven already."

"Have I seen her before? It seems that I have seen her before."

"Does he remember ever having left the clearing?"

"No."

"Then he may remember that visions may or may not be true."

"But it is true that today we'll be in Wolverham. And it is true that today I will see the king."

"So Lord Tousle should have something fitting to wear." Da took from his pocket a square-linked golden chain and held it in a shaft of morning sun, gleaming dully. I jumped from the bench and helped him clamber up, and standing behind me, he fastened it around my neck. "He shall wear it until he knows when to give it away," he said, his voice quiet, a little saddened.

"I could never give away something you have given me."

"He will give it away when there is need," Da answered.

12

He had never before given me anything like it. A new jerkin, a knife, a plow, yes. The tethered ball we struck together, the bright paper frame we lofted to the wind like a rainbow in the sky, certainly. But never something like this chain. The weight of it surprised me. It lay cold and sharp against my chest, and somehow its giving turned the morning solemn.

"So," Da said, and leapt down. "Shall Tousle and Da go or stay? There is still the splitting to do, and then there's the spinning all to begin." He pulled up his beard and fingered the tip of it. "And there's the noontime blizzard to mind."

"Da, we're to Wolverham."

He considered. "Yes, I suppose. The splitting will keep. As for the spinning . . ." He snapped the fingers of his left hand, and the wheel sprung around, hesitated once, then whirled into a smooth circle. "Four skeins, maybe five before the snow begins," he instructed.

"There will be no snow!"

I hurried Da through breakfast, and while the bowls doused and dried themselves, I fetched the horses. By the time I led them saddled and eager from the barn, Da had finished with the hamper we were to take. I hustled him out of the house and hefted him onto the Gray, adjusting the girth beneath him and loosening it again when the buckle snagged his beard.

"Tousle and Da will be there"—I led his left foot into the stirrup—"when they will be there," he fussed. I ignored him, guided the right foot into the other stirrup, tied the hamper behind his saddle, then leapt up onto the Dapple.

"Da, which way?" I called, the Dapple pulling at the bit and tossing his head back and forth. He could never forget that he had once been a colt.

"A moment, a moment. He's in such a blessed hurry. Wolverham will wait through the day."

"Da, the procession . . ."

"No doubt the king himself will wait for Tousle's arrival." And turning around, he blinked his eyes at the house. The door closed and fastened itself, and the shutters banged together across the windows. "Now," he said, "to Wolverham."

Da glided his hand across the clearing and toward the dark woods. I held my breath—and held it, and held it. And then the trees shoved themselves aside, wallowing with their deep roots in earth, their boughs waving gracefully to scent the air. A pine-needle path stretched slowly like a yawning cat between the trees, stretching and stretching until it fell down a small hill and was lost to sight. Neither the Dapple nor the Gray needed any urging.

The clearing was unbound.

It was cold and soft under the trees, the last of winter's snow as powdery as flour. It blew off the pine needles as we approached, so that we moved without a sound except for the steamy snorting of the Dapple, who was glad to be out and eager to show it. I let him have his head, and we trotted, the trees just ahead of us backing away as we approached, then clasping their boughs together and closing behind us.

Suddenly the trunks shoved back more quickly, and with a rush the Gray galloped by, Da leaning close to his neck and laughing for all the world. "And Tousle so anxious to get to Wolverham," he hollered over his shoulder. I spurred the Dapple, but the trees rushed in close and narrow behind Da, and there was no room to pass.

"Hardly fair," I yelled, but Da pretended he had not heard.

We rollicked down the hillsides, the air so fiercely cold I could hardly breathe. It seared my lungs, but still I hollered and laughed and hollered again, all the while hearing Da's hooting and hooting, and the Gray's hooves flinging snow and dirt in my face so I was always spitting it out and pulling back. I pressed the Dapple, but the trees never opened enough for me to pass until we reached the lowland, and the woods threaded themselves out to fields and meadows. Da waited for me to catch up with him, his face red and glowing, his beard flung back over his shoulder. "There's a balance, he should know, between letting a horse have his way and guiding him. It takes experience to find such a balance. He'll never win a race unless he finds it." Da grinned.

"When you set the trees to keep me from a pass . . ."

"Well, if he must find an excuse, there is that." He laughed.

"And you've been this way before. You must have, since you know the path."

"To Wolverham and back."

"I suppose you've been to the castle itself, Da."

"On occasion."

"Perhaps you've seen the king and queen. The doors opened before you and the guards bowed you into their august presence. You knelt to them, and they promised you great rewards if you would perform a great service."

"Something close to that."

I laughed a cloud into the cold air. "Da, you've never been to the castle, much less seen the king and queen. Never in your life."

Da winked over at me. "Tousle might try to imagine for a moment—I know that this is difficult, but he might try to imagine anyway—that there is something in this wide, wide world that he does not know."

"The Gray will sprout wings before I believe you've been to the castle."

"Then he will be plucking horsehair from the clouds before long."

The Gray and the Dapple ambled along companionably. It was warmer down in the lowland, and though spring was still a time away, the fields were turning their dark selves to soak up the sunlight. Some of the fields were already furrowed, and we passed a cart laden with the winter's manure moving up and down the rows, drawn by thick horses. I pulled back on the Dapple to watch: I had never seen such fields, and the work of them, the sheer hard work of them, thrilled me.

"Come fall, the gold wheat of these fields will be brighter than a winter sun," Da whispered. "Tousle will see." The farmer seemed to hear us and waved cheerfully.

The first building we passed that morning was a low mossy inn, where coachmen waited patiently for travelers sleeping late. They too waved to us, and I waved back, awkward, realizing with a start that I had never before waved to anyone other than Da. "The fresh morning of the world," they called, and I smiled and waved again, not sure how to answer them.

Now farmhouses started to scatter themselves in the fields, blue smoke rising straight and quick in the cold, still air, their stuccoed sides covered with vines that would soon leaf out. As we rode on, they settled themselves closer and closer together, until I could have called from the window of one and been heard over at the other. In one yard ducks and geese waddled and cackled in the bright light, gathering around a farm girl spreading feed from out her apron—a real farm girl, not just one of Da's pictures in the air. I waved to her, but she did not see me.

"The fresh morning of the world," I hollered.

She turned to look, smiled shyly, and then went back to her sowing.

I watched her until the road bent us away.

We passed a low cottage whose walls leaned in to hold each other up. No waddling and cackling here. It was a yard full of puddles and yellow mud. The stone walls of the mill beside it were still covered with white ice, and the mill wheel groaned at its turning as if it could barely make its way through the river water. It looked to be a frozen, hard world that these people lived in, and when a woman stooped out from the cottage, carting a yoke with buckets over her shoulders, she did not look up as I called to her.

"Da," I said, "must she carry those herself?"

"She must."

"And us sitting here watching her."

Da said nothing, and I slipped off the Dapple and ran through stained puddles to her. "Mother, let me carry those for you on this fresh morning of the world."

She turned her face up to me from underneath the yoke, and I was startled by the washed-out gray of her eyes, and by the sharpness of the cheekbones that looked ready to knife through the skin. I reached over and took the buckets from her, wondering how long it had been since someone had done a kindness for this old woman. She pointed to the open water, and I took the buckets, one in each hand, and knelt down to the river. Here the turning of the wheel was so loud I could not speak to her, the spray of it freezing on my face as I dragged the black water up.

Together we walked back to the cottage. She turned at the doorway and reached out for the water. "I've nothing to—"

She stopped and held out her hand as if to touch my cheek.

"What is it, Mother?"

Her outstretched finger, gnarled and bunched, pulled back. Then she shook her head. "An old woman's fancy. That's all that is left. An old woman's fancy." She took the buckets from me, and with a look of such longing that all the wealth of the East could not fill it, she turned and went inside.

Slowly I climbed back up the Dapple. "Hers is a lonely, hard life."

"There's the miller to keep it with her."

"But there's a coldness about that place. It looks like it lost something a long time ago."

"It does," Da said quietly. "Like the queen."

On to Wolverham. Soon others joined us on the road, walking with slung packs, or riding in carts or on jaunty horses. It seemed as if all the kingdom were draining into Wolverham to see the procession of the king. The Gray and the Dapple caught the excitement, and we had to hold their heads tightly.

"Once we're in town, what shall we do, Da?"

"Tousle should go to the castle to see if their majesties are ready to receive him."

"Da."

"If not, then they'll find a spot to see the king's procession, and after that, the day will unfold itself as it will." A vision of the procession came over me. It would be grander than anything I had ever seen. Horses and banners, trumpets and armored knights, pageant wagons and cavalry—I imagined them all marching to echoing cheers, cheers that would join with the blaring trumpets, neighing horses, and thundering hooves to deafen me.

"He is grinning," said Da.

"I suppose."

"He looks like a lunatic, grinning at nothing."

"You look like a madman, scowling at everything."

"Then there's a fair pair," he called, and swatted at me.

The first sight of the gates of Wolverham did not disappoint. Long yellow streamers flowed in the breeze, lofting and sinking with the air. The arches were larger than our whole house, taller than most trees I had seen, and as we drew near and felt the press of the crowd, they loomed round and open and grand. Once beneath them, I hunched down under the terrible press of weight held up by the arch's invisible hand. I reined the Dapple in and looked up to where the stones rounded into a perfect curve, marveling that they should not fall.

Ahead of me, Da turned around. "If he stops there long enough, that fellow behind him—the one with the manure cart—will dump his load in a place neither had expected."

I pressed the Dapple out from the shadow of the gates and came to the edge of the town square of Wolverham. I suppose my mouth gaped. Da shook his head at me and whispered, "Like a lunatic," but I could not care. It was bigger and noisier and smellier and grander than I had ever imagined. I slipped off the Dapple and balanced on the solid roundness of cobblestones. The clatter of carts and the ringing of horseshoes filled the air. Merchants cried out, hawking ducks, butchered pigs, last fall's turnips and apples, embroidered clothes "from faraway Cathay." The spiced scents of roasted sweetmeats wafted from small fires and mingled with other smells that had more to do with barns.

"He should close his mouth," Da said. "First, to livery the horses. Across the square there. And then, to eat." I took the reins of the two horses and led them to a stable that charged a fee so high that even the stableman grimaced with the saying of it.

"So much, then?"

"So much on the day of a procession."

Da scooped up some dirt, clenched his hand, shook it once, and dropped two silver coins into the hand of the startled stableman. "There will be two, perhaps three more come evening."

"When you'll find the horses curried and fed, sir," the stableman answered, "better than if you and the boy were to do it yourselves."

We left the Dapple and the Gray nuzzling an unexpected portion of oats—and the stableman digging frantically at the dirt where Da had stood—and soon Da was juggling hot sweetmeats in his hands and I was following with the hamper. We sat at the edge of the square, Da squeezing honey from the comb onto his brown bread and pouring hot cider from a jug, me burning the tip of my tongue on the sweetmeats, but mostly just watching as we ate. Day after day these smells, these sounds, these people filled the square. And they filled it without me. Day after day.

When he finished his brown bread, Da pulled up his beard and checked it for crumbs. Then he plucked his pipe from his vest pocket.

"Da, the procession!"

"The king will not wait for a smoke?"

I stood. Da sighed, and started to fuss with the hamper.

"Da, we'll be late."

"Then Tousle should take this to the livery, and by the time he is back, he'll . . ."

But I did not wait to hear. I pushed through the square with the hamper, left it with the stableman—he was still digging for coins—pushed back through the square, grabbed Da's hand—"But the pipe is just lit!"—and soon we were jostling for a place on the broad way that stretched from the square to the castle. The crowd was so thick that I walked in front to keep Da from being trampled. I had not imagined what it would be like to have so many bodies pressed against me. And all the while, far ahead down the way, the massive stones of the castle rose like a mountain, tier after tier into the sky.

We found a place on the rise of an arched bridge spanning a small rivulet and stood with our elbows out to fend off the crowds. At the sound of trumpets, we craned our necks down the way, and I leaned out to be the first to see.

It was all as I had hoped—and much more. Banners sprang high, and I could hear the battering of the iron-shod horses. The crowd throated its cheers, so loud that the very stones of the bridge rang to them.

Da took me by the elbow. "He must remember what the procession is for."

"Of course, Da. For the king." I shouted so that he might hear me. More trumpets sounded, with notes high and clear and so piercing that it seemed as if they must crack the glassy blue of the sky. I leaned out even farther, but I still could not see anything but crowds and the high banners.

"Tousle is not quite right."

"For the king's victory over the rebels." But I could

hardly listen to Da, for suddenly the feathered helmets of the first horsemen waved over the crowd.

"For the king's victory over those who rebelled against Lord Beryn," Da corrected. "He must listen to me now. No, to me. Listen. The rebellion was against Lord Beryn."

"Yes, Lord Beryn, the first of the Great Lords. I know. There, Da, the cavalry. Can you see?" The sun mirrored their silver armor, and reflections from it danced merrily against the houses that fronted the avenue.

But Da was not listening. He reached up with both hands and pulled my face down toward him. "Nothing is ever quite by chance. What spins out now took its place on the wheel long ago. Does he understand? Does Tousle understand?"

"Da," I said, "the procession."

I think he sighed. It was hard to tell, with the sounding trumpets. But he held on to me and spoke once more. "Our home on the hillside: let it come back to him now and again."

And then the procession was upon us, louder than glory, brighter than song. While the glittering cavalry passed, trumpets silvered the sunlight. After the trumpets, foot soldiers strutted past, gleaming lances held to the sky, blue coverlets fringed with gold slapping from the tips. Then the king's stable: white horses groomed to the ideal, their manes and tails ribboned with golden thread, their hooves polished to shiny horn, their eyes red and nostrils flared.

And on the largest of these horses the king himself, in bright golden armor crested with feathers whiter than nature had ever conceived. He held his arms out to his people, and I cheered and hollered and pressed forward to touch the sunlit, golden king. He seemed to carry the light of the day on his shoulders.

Just behind him came the twelve Great Lords, robed in ermine, riding on twelve piebald steeds. Lord Beryn rode first, the crowd calling out his name when they saw him. He moved through the cheering air like a proud statue, oblivious to those around him. So too the other eleven lords, so proud, so powerful that they would not look beneath them. Their horses strained at the reins, but the stone hands of the Great Lords held them in check, so even the jeweled rings that fell from their lordly ears hung perfectly straight and still.

They pulled after them Lord Beryn's own Guard, knights mounted on stern, high-stepping horses. With swords unsheathed and held upright, they seemed a small forest of glittering steel, and the crowd drew back from them as they would from a loosely chained wild animal. The tunics that covered their armor were bright white, with no ensign.

Then I stood on my toes to watch for the queen. And when I saw her, I knew that Da's misty vision had been just right. She rode on a piebald palfrey, and she too did not look at the crowd. Her eyes were always to her hands on the reins, and so quiet and small she looked after the golden king that the crowd stilled. She wore her ermine robes like a costume that did not fit, and the silver diadem that flashed from her hair seemed duller than it should be. I wanted to call to her, but I somehow feared to. I suddenly thought how beautiful she might look baking brown bread.

She passed, and the crowd began to cheer anew.

For behind her came the king's servants, themselves clothed in gold-threaded capes, bags of coins at their hips. They scattered silver and gold to the crowd as the cheers doubled, tripled, as hands reached to catch the king's coin.

One fell at my feet, but before I could bend to grab it, those nearby had leapt at it and bloodied their knuckles with reaching.

Then more trumpets, more foot soldiers—the king's guard this time, with red coverlets and lions rampant. The cheers were becoming throaty and hoarse.

"It is grand. Isn't it grand, Da?" I called, but I did not look to see if he had heard. "The king must be the greatest, richest man in the world."

But the procession was not yet over.

chapter two

A black horse creased through the crowd, his muzzle taut over yellow teeth. On his back the brawniest of men rode high, clothed all in black. A black hood draped over his head, but the steel of his eyes showed through slits, as cold as if he could have skewered us all before breakfast and then sat down to eggs and meat without washing the blood away. He rode like Fear, one mailed hand holding the reins tightly, the other grasping a coiled whip.

Besotted soldiers came behind him, wearing dented and stained armor, mismatched and hugger-mugger in their marching. At first I thought that the boos and catcalls echoing down the way were for them, but they were not. The crowd was calling to those they led: the rebels.

A hundred men and women staggered behind the soldiers, their faces looking down at their manacled hands, their feet fettered to a shuffle. Except for the clanking of their chains, the prisoners made no sounds. The men kept to the outside, shielding the women from the rubbish that the crowd threw. But they could do little to protect them.

The crowd beside me cupped fetid mud from the rivulet and lashed it at them. Those watching from upstairs windows along the route spilled worse.

"Scum to scum!"

"Stinking rebels! Traitors!"

They did stink. A stench moved with them in the close air of the street. A stench of contamination and of the blood their bare feet left on the road. The crowd hated them the more for the smell. They hated them for the blood.

I stared, stunned, as the rebels trudged against their chains, some dodging the refuse being thrown, others with eyes closed, too exhausted to dodge. They were all gray and red and tattered. They moved hopelessly into hopelessness.

Except one.

At the very end of the crowd walked a boy who looked to be almost my age, his arms held protectively around two young girls. Most of his shirt was torn from him, and he was covered with filth. A rock had cut his forehead, and blood that he could not wipe away had dried across his face. The soldiers swaggering behind prodded him forward with bloodied lances, and though he stumbled, he walked as erect as he could, striding as far as his chains—and the young girls—would allow, ignoring the howls that flew at him like demons.

And he was blind. Below the bloody dark hair that fell down his forehead, a terrible slash cut across his eyes and sealed them with scars.

The inside of my gut wrenched at the sight, and I vomited into the rivulet, vomited until I could hardly breathe, hoping all the while that I would vomit out the sight of the blinded eyes.

But I could not.

The procession passed by, and the crowd surged onto the way, pushing me like a mountain avalanche, as irresistible as nightfall. "Da, Da," I sputtered, half panicked for myself, half panicked that Da would be crushed. But no matter how far I craned my neck, I could not see him, and with the roar of the crowd, I could not hope to hear him. So, shouldered and shoved, I was herded along, swears and curses louder than blaring trumpets in my ears, until at last the way opened up into a wide courtyard. There the castle, darker and more shadowed than I had first seen it, crouched under the clouds scuttling across the sky, the high wind tearing at the banners.

Here the soldiers stretched out in a double line, their lances holding the crowd back. The rebels leaned wearily against one another, shivering. Some fell to the ground. But the blind boy still stood and still held the two girls close to him, his bare back taking the brunt of the wind.

Above them—above us all—trumpeters marched to the edge of a high parapet. As one, they lifted their brassy horns to the dark sky and sounded a single clear note. When it died away, the golden king stepped forward. Though he had dismounted, he looked somehow even larger. The Great Lords moved into a half circle around him, and just outside the circle the queen waited. The king paused until they were all in place, like an actor waiting for a cue. We all felt the moment. The crowd fell to an absolute silence. The clouds stopped their scuttling. And then he spoke, and the wind sprang up to carry the frost of his breath.

"Is there a greater crime than to rebel against one's king? Is there a greater crime than to rebel against the one appointed by God himself to rule? As there is one God, there is one ruler. As there is one God, there is one king. And if lords loyal to that king rule over you, is not obedience to the lords obedience to the king? And is not rebellion against them rebellion against him? And when those rulers are beneficent, caring, and wise—when the king watches over his subjects as a father watches over his children—how much worse is it to rebel? How much worse to leave what is ordained, as unnatural as a river leaving its proper bed?"

The light waned from the sky as the clouds sucked it into their darkness, but still the golden king glowed. The light seemed to come from inside him, but it shone on no one else.

"To rebel against Lord Beryn, to rebel against any of my Great Lords, is to rebel against me, your God-appointed sovereign. A rebellion so unnatural can lead to only a single just sentence. As a flooded river must be stemmed, so also must rebellion. And you—you loyal people of Wolverham— you must pronounce the single just sentence." He held his golden-mailed hands out over the courtyard as if to bless us, and in the quiet that followed, the wind dropped as if it too would hear the sentence of Wolverham.

Then, just behind me, the first voice cried out: "Death!"

"Death to the traitors and rebels all!"

"Hanging! Hang the rebels!"

The golden king stood with his arms outstretched, and he drew the words out of our guts and into our mouths. The cries grew louder and then joined together, a stampede of wild sound trampling through the courtyard, pummeling through the air with horrid bluntness. I felt it square against me. I opened my own mouth, felt the words rush into it, and . . . and then I saw the face of the blind boy turn to me. Through his scarred eyelids he looked at me, and my words charred before they were spoken.

But all around me the terrible cry went on and on until the sky itself must crack.

"Da," I called, "Da," but he was not there.

Another single trumpet note and the king lowered his hands, the cries lowering with them. "Death, then. You, the loyal people of Wolverham, have decreed it, and your king bows to your will. Death to all traitors. Death to all rebels."

Another blast from the trumpets, answered by screams that struck the ear like tongs.

The king raised his hands again. "But God is a merciful, charitable God. I am a merciful, charitable king. And you are a merciful, charitable people. Is there one among you who would hinder the death of these rebels? Is there a voice among you that would plead for mercy? Are there any that would cry for this brood of—"

"No. Not a one," came a voice from behind me.

"No one. No one," echoed the crowd, louder and louder, faster and faster, until the words were lost in a cataclysm of sound.

The darkness of the clouds was almost complete, matted to a fuzzy thickness torn at the edges. Then one loosed its hold and snow fell, white and dry, falling with a stillness that stilled the crowd.

And in that stillness the queen stepped forward toward the golden king. "Majesty," she said quietly, "I will plead."

Silence in that great courtyard. Absolute silence, as if there had never been a single word spoken in all the world.

The king stared long at the queen. Then he turned to Lord Beryn, who had moved closer to him, his hand hard upon his sword. The other Great Lords glowered, and one swore with words that should never sound near a queen.

Slowly the king faced us again, the golden light still bright. But when he spoke, I knew beyond all doubt that he was afraid. I saw terror clutch at him like a vampire.

"The voice of one against so many," he called out, his voice quavering just a little. "Is there another of you, people of Wolverham? Is there another who would stand with the rebels, linking himself to that unnatural crime?"

The boy's closed eyes were still upon me. Upon me! The scar across them seemed no barrier.

"Another who would plead for rebels?"

I moved before I even thought of moving, as if I were in a dream. It felt as if I were simply taking on my own part, like another actor stepping onto the stage to perform his appointed role. The crowd fell away, and in the quiet of the snow, I walked across the courtyard and up the steps to the edge of the parapet. The king stared at me with such surprise and, I realized, such hatred, it might almost have been better had he struck me down. But the invisible vampire was still clutching him.

I hardly knew what to say, what part to play. With every eye in Wolverham upon me—and with the face of the blind boy turned toward me—I lowered my knees in front of the king, bowed my head, and felt a hand grip my heart.

"Your Majesty," I said quietly, "I plead for them."

A long silence. I waited to hear the call of Da, but it never came.

"You plead for them?" came the king's voice instead, icicles in every word. "You plead for them? Who are you to move my just anger, or the decrees of all Wolverham?"

"Tousle, Majesty."

"Tousle," spat the king. "Tousle. Your plea suggests that you yourself are one of them—a traitor to your king."

"Majesty," I said slowly, looking up while the cold pricked the back of my neck, "I am not. I know they have rebelled against Lord Beryn, and so against you. I know that I have nothing to exchange for your mercy. But I plead for it anyway."

At that moment the queen took a step forward, so that she was in front of the Great Lords. Her eyes locked onto mine, as though she might tie me to her. And she had. I wanted to leap up and run into her arms, like one who suddenly knows that he has missed something for a very long time, without knowing what it was he missed.

"Good sir," she said to the king, though still looking at me, "the boy pleads for nothing but mercy for others."

"For rebels."

"Majesty is never diminished by grace," she replied.

Da's words. Da's very words. As if the queen had heard them too and was speaking them out as her part in the play. But she was no actor, and this was no play.

"Grace and pleas are misplaced when given to traitors."

"They are pleas that you yourself invited."

"You play with words, lady. It is beneath you."

"A peasant's trick," said Lord Beryn, stepping beside her.

"Then I will play no more. I plead with the boy." And her hand reached out, quivering, to touch my shoulder. I felt its weight and heat.

The world halted. The king, the Great Lords, the rebels—all the world was frozen except for me and the queen. We lived in the heat from her hand. Nothing else was real, and if the world had never moved again, I would have been content to hold still for that eternal moment.

But the world did move again.

"Lady," the king's voice rumbled low, "you stand here at

my behest, and at my behest only." His eyes glanced back to Lord Beryn. "It is not your place to plead with the boy." Reluctantly she withdrew her hand from my shoulder, and I grew colder. "Your place is to do my will, and that will is your return to Saint Eynsham Abbey within the hour."

Slowly the queen stepped back, but her eyes never left mine.

The king turned to me again.

"You say you have nothing to exchange for my mercy."

"Nothing, Majesty."

"And I will not give you freely the life of a traitor— assuming you are none yourself."

"I am not, Majesty."

"So you must find something in exchange. Something of equal or even greater value."

The sense that this was all a play came upon me again. And I would act the part.

"Majesty," I said loudly, "tell me what it is you wish."

At my reply a single cheer came from the crowd, a woman's call startling in the stillness of the growing snow. And then another came, and another.

With a sweep of his armored hand, the king struck me across the face. I fell backward, tumbling down the stairs to the courtyard.

"No, lady, you will stay there," I heard the king yell. Murmurs rose from the crowd like smoke. "Let it be understood now," the king called loudly, "that no one is to assist this boy on his journey to the gallows. Noble, peasant, freeman, or slave. No one, on pain of taking his place."

I looked back above me; the king stood poised, one arm pointing to me, the other to the crowd. The snow was now falling thick and heavy, and when I spat the blood that had sprung into my mouth, the red of the spittle was bright on the whitened ground. I rose to my knees.

The king turned to the queen. "You, madam, will make the preparations for your return to Saint Eynsham. See to it that they are made quickly, or your next holiday will find age stooping your shoulders." He motioned at me. "Bring the boy."

One of the king's guards left the rebels and gripped me above my elbow. Half shoving, half lifting, he thrust me back up the stairs, onto the parapet, and into the wake left by the king and the Great Lords, a wake that drew me into the mouth of the castle.

The cobblestones of the courtyard gave way to stone slabs. Through a door, and then we were crossing on blood-red marble. Another door, and we were on filigreed rugs thicker than the thickest moss. Each of the hallways grew brighter and brighter, each boasting more and more curious gilt devices and decorated with gold urns and plates and statues burnished to a brightness. Yet another door, quite heavy this time, and the guard tossed me lightly into a room bright with fire. Braided ropes and coils of thin gold hung in loops from the walls, like whips ready at hand. A great blaze burned in the center of the room, the flames reflecting in the coils. The gold dazzled, and I shut my eyes against it.

We waited there for a long time, as the fire burned low, the room chilled, and the golden coils grew darker. Servants came to set lanterns on the walls, and still we waited, the guard standing wordlessly with his hand on his swordhilt, and me crouched by the waning fire, wondering how it was that I had come here, and thinking, strangely enough, of brown bread and hot cider, of the Dapple and the Gray, of the home on the hillside. Of Da.

A hoarse call, and the guard pulled me up and shoved me on into a grand room, warmer and brighter than any I had been in before. Here the walls were paneled with gold, and the ceiling mosaic glowed with the metal. The lanterns shone from golden brocades, and even the floor was inlaid with gold and ebony squares.

The king stood behind a long trestle table crowded with golden platters of steaming meat and stew, with golden flagons of wine, with golden bowls that spilled fruit. The Great Lords sat on either side of the king, most of them gesturing to the servants, who were coming from behind tapestries and scurrying about.

The guard pushed me to the front of the table, then stepped back so I was alone, facing the king. He stared at me, and I saw then that his eyes were so pale they were almost white.

"Boy," said the king, "you have nothing you might exchange for the life of these rebels?"

"Nothing, Your Majesty."

"And do you regret that you meddled in affairs that were not yours to meddle in?"

The Great Lords had now turned to me, some for the sport but at least one with interest.

"It is too late for regret, Majesty," I said.

Guffaws from the Great Lords.

"So it is," said the king. "Much too late."

"Majesty," said Lord Beryn, "there is no gain for us in dealing so with this boy. Have him whipped and thrown from the castle, and we will turn to more important matters." He held up a great shank of meat, and at this the other Great Lords laughed.

"Lord Beryn," answered the king without looking at

him, "let us give this boy something to exchange." He leaned forward over the table, and when he spoke, there was a sudden earnestness to his voice. "Boy, I give you a riddle. Its answer is the life of the rebels. And your own. Do you understand?"

"I do, Majesty."

"Then listen well: *What fills a hand fuller than a skein of gold?*"

Again the Great Lords laughed. They seemed no longer to be the lordly statues who had processed to the castle; now they were red and fleshy, their jowls leaping with their merriment, two or three sputtering out the wine from their mouths.

But Lord Beryn was not laughing. He stared at the king, and his face was hard and thoughtful. With one hand he twirled the rings on his fingers.

Nor did the king laugh. He stood leaning toward me, and I saw that this was no mere riddle for him, that there was more here than he would say. In the midst of the gold and the laughter, I saw in his pale eyes a strange and even urgent pleading, as if the vampire were still in the room. As if he hoped that I could save him.

"Majesty," said Lord Beryn, "this is folly. The boy is a lunatic. Send him away, or dress him in motley and have him play the fool for us." More laughter from the Great Lords. More red wine poured into gold flagons, some spilling on the white damask cloth.

"If it be folly, Lord Beryn, it is folly on my head and mine alone. We will send the boy to bring back the riddle's answer."

Surprised and angry, Lord Beryn rose to stand beside the king. I was amazed at how large he was. His shoulders topped the king's head, and the black hair that bearded him made the king look almost like a boy. "Any number of answers will do for such a riddle," he growled. "It is folly to do what you are doing."

"Only one answer will do," insisted the king.

Lord Beryn grunted and turned to me. His hand reached out across the table like a bear's, and grabbing my shirt, he yanked me to him. "And is this the boy to find the answer, then?" He looked at me and laughed. "This puny boy, to answer a king's riddle?" The Great Lords roared.

And then, suddenly, Lord Beryn was staring at the chain Da had put around my neck, then at my face, then back at the chain. His own face was a contortion. Then, with a rough pull, he covered the chain with my shirt.

"Majesty," Lord Beryn said, "perhaps your first thought was the best. Perhaps this boy does indeed show himself the rebel, and he should be held."

"Rebel or not, he will have his chance to solve the riddle. There is the king's word on it."

"Then, my lord, let me add my merriment to the issue." Another Great Lord rose—already he swayed with drink—and motioned to the soldier who had led me in. He whispered into his ear, swaying the while, and in a moment the soldier was gone.

"My lord," began the king, and he looked at me—and his look was anxious.

"Allow this one merriment, Majesty. Just this one." The Great Lord paused, cleared his throat, winked at Lord Beryn, and swallowed a gulp of wine. "If we are to send a boy to learn the answer to the riddle, then he must go with a companion. One suited to guide and to lead. One who will help him seek out that which is hidden."

Another of the grinning Great Lords stood, holding his overflowing cup above his head. "One to tread the lonely road beside him. One to ease his way in the darkness."

Yet another stood, holding his cup high too, but the Great Lords dissolved into guffaws when he fell backward over his chair. He staggered up, lifted his cup again, and called, "One to . . ."

But he never finished, for the laughter of the other Great Lords rose to a shriek when the soldier dragged the blind boy into the room. The golden walls echoed with their spewing, echoed with their rollicking guffaws. When the soldier pulled at the chains so that the boy sprawled to the floor, their laughter deafened. I knelt down and held him by the shoulders. "Well," he said, so quietly that only I could hear, "at least I am out of the snow."

But Lord Beryn again did not laugh; instead, he turned with thunder to the drunken lord. "Of all the boys to choose, you choose this one. Fool. And again a fool." He looked at the blind boy, then turned to the king. "This smacks of design. You must end this whim, this prank."

"It is neither whim nor prank," answered the king, and turned back to me. "Seven days," he said. "You both have seven days to find the answer to this riddle. If you do not return by the morning after the seventh day, the rebels will hang and you two be declared outlaw and hunted down with dogs. It is an answer you must find."

"By the morning after the seventh day," I answered, "we will return with the riddle's answer."

"This one will keep the time!" another of the Great Lords scoffed, pointing at the blind boy. All the other lords careened into laughter again as the boy stood by me silently. He looked ahead as though he could see, and the king's eyes never left his face.

With a scoff of disgust Lord Beryn threw his hands into the air. "Fool," he cried again, and the floor vibrated with his stomping. But at a sign from the king, the guard grabbed both of us and dragged us through the lighted rooms, until once again we were on the parapet. He unlocked the chains from the blind boy's wrists, who winced at the sores that had formed there. "If it had been my choice, it would have been better to slit open your throats now," snarled the guard, and with his foot he shoved first me, then the blind boy, down the stairs and into the courtyard.

The snowfall had thickened while we had been in the castle, and only a few of the crowd still remained. They cast long looks at us, afraid to approach because of the king's warning but curious nonetheless. The soldiers, grumbling and cursing the cold, were prodding the rebels into a tighter and tighter group until they sat huddled against each other, the snow covering them and the wind tearing out racking coughs from their throats.

I looked through the snow for Da, but he was not there. Shivering and wet, I knew he must come. He must.

But he did not, and suddenly I felt my eyes welling. It seemed that this morning—this day I had waited for—had been a lifetime and more ago. Now I was carrying a death sentence. If only I might find Da, I could drop it like a weight and ride back home.

And then I looked at the rebels, and at the two young girls who watched the blind boy so closely, and knew I could not.

"I'm not the best one to judge direction," said the boy, "but I do think that we might choose any rather than stay here."

"Any that lead from the castle," I agreed. "For now. But we will be back here after seven days."

"We will." He nodded. He turned to the rebels. "Seven days. We will be back after seven days." At his call, the two girls clasped each other tightly.

"It would be best to go back to the horses," I said.

"Horses?" He held out his hand to stop me. "I don't ride horses. They're afraid of me."

"They're afraid of you?"

"They are."

"You're sure of this?"

"Yes."

"These are very gentle horses."

"They would have to tell me so themselves, if they expected me to ride them."

I took him by the elbow and, holding my arm across my face, walked down the deserted way in the growing darkness. We kept our faces from the wind that cut at us, but I looked as much as I could for Da. Perhaps he had gone back for the horses and was waiting at the stalls. "Not far," I called, and the blind boy nodded in return.

But Da was not at the stables. Neither were the Dapple and the Gray. The stableman was there alone, boiling a stew over his forge. The steam of it rose in the horsey air.

"My da has been back for the horses?" I asked.

The stableman looked me up and down.

"Who are you, then?"

"My da and I stabled our horses here this morning. The Dapple and the Gray. Just this very morning. For two silver coins."

"Boy, I have been at this forge since before dawn. Well before. And in all that time there's not been one single horse brought here. Not a single one, the pity of it."

"That's a lie," I cried, and his face hardened. He set down the wooden spoon that had been stirring the stew and picked up a long column of black iron from the fire, glowing yellow-white at the tip.

"You'd best be careful about your words, boy."

"My da and I brought in two horses this morning. The Dapple and the Gray. We stabled them there, and you filled up their troughs from the feed box behind you."

The stableman moved aside. "There's no feed box behind me, boy. You brought no horses in here. And as for silver coins—I haven't seen one outside the king's pocket in a dozen years." I looked into the stables; they were empty except for the cobwebs that stretched across their corners. It had been a long time since a horse had stood there.

"Away with you both. Do you think I don't know what you're about? You smell good food and concoct a story to get at it. Away with you."

"There must be another livery nearby," suggested the boy.

"No other," said the stableman. "Now be off. I don't mind spitting a couple of boys, especially just before my dinner." He twirled the poker in his hands.

I took the boy's elbow and backed away, the stableman following and thrusting the hot iron to hurry us along. We backed into the street, and the wind and snow struck us full in our backs as he barred and bolted the door.

Darkness fell with all its heavy weight. The wet of sloppy snow. Silence. Awful silence.

"We'd best find a place out of the wind, some alley," the boy said.

I looked around almost panicked, still half expecting Da to step out of the dark. "It's impossible to see anything in this snow," I cried.

He did not answer, and I felt a sudden shame come upon me.

"This way," I said, taking his elbow again, and the wind shrieked us down past the livery, past closed shops, past lighted houses, and finally to the cold granite portico of what must be a nobleman's house. We backed ourselves into an angle of the wall, hunched down, and shivered into each other.

"It would be good to know each other's names before we freeze to death," I chattered. "Mine's Tousle."

"Innes," he answered, "and we won't be freezing to death. Not when there's the riddle to be solved."

I closed my eyes and then began to laugh. Innes poked at me. "The snow is coming down and us barely out of it, lying against stone as frozen as the north wind itself, and you're laughing. You must be either a lunatic or a madman."

"No, no. Neither of those. It's just that I've been waiting for this day for as long as I can remember."

"Well," he said, "next time wait for a day with better weather." Then he pressed his chin to his chest and tried to fall into sleep.

chapter three

A sheet of water came cascading toward us, and my mouth opened wide to warn Innes—just in time for it to dash in and set me gagging. After having shivered through most of the dark, it seemed too hard that we should be wet through now.

"Beggars at our doors! At our very doors!" outraged a voice above us. "Off with you. Off with you! You'll not be sleeping here!"

We both stood, me still coughing. My head was fusty, and I was so cold that my legs would hardly straighten. I held my hands up; they trembled.

"You're the boy who— Off with you both, before I set the dogs out."

Innes turned his face to the voice above us. "How large are the dogs?"

"Innes," I whispered, "are dogs afraid of you too?"

"Terrified." He smiled.

I looked up. "You don't need to set the dogs on us," I called. "We're not about to rob and murder you."

"Rob and murder is what the king would do if he found you sleeping at my doorstep. I'll not be risking it."

"A loaf of bread, then," asked Innes, "to see us on our way?"

The shutters clapped to with a startling crack, and as I looked down the narrow street, I saw that all the shutters were tight. The houses looked fearful in the pale light of the heatless sun.

Back home there was oatmeal and cinnamon. Warm milk and down quilts. And hot embers. But here I could feel my wet clothes stiffening with the cold, and my stomach made sounds no stomach should ever make.

"I think we should try to get back to my da's house," I said. "Da will be sure to be there."

"Is it far?"

"Far enough. He must have gone, and taken the horses back."

"We still have the riddle."

"Da will solve it. There's not a single day that goes by without him setting a riddle."

Innes nodded slowly. "There's no making a mistake. You are sure he can solve it?"

"With one eye closed," I said, then stopped and put my hand to my face. "Innes, I'm sorry. That was ..."

But he waved it away. "If your da cannot solve it with one eye closed, I'll solve it with two. Now, with both yours open, can you find the city gates before the dogs come out?"

We tottered past the houses, the shops, the livery, and came again into the square. Walking out of that quiet street and into the square was like walking out of a quiet barn into a storm: You turn the corner, and the suddenness of the noise smacks at you like a flail.

The square was as full as it had been yesterday, as if the procession had never happened. Cart horses had already tramped the new snow into slush, and plashing cart wheels were showering icy water against the merchant stalls. There was all the clamor and bantering and sheer cackle of the place, but it was nothing to me beside the smells that scented the air: sausages, sweetmeats, bacon rinds, pork roasts.

"And bread," said Innes. "Smell the heat of it."

Together we stepped out into it all . . . and suddenly everything was as quiet as a deserted chancel.

A farmwife haggling over the freshness of her late-fall turnips saw us—and stilled. The clothier hawking his Persian silks froze as if the air had iced around him. Even a beggar, hugging his tatters close to himself and holding out a gnarled palm, quieted his endless plea at the sight of us.

We walked through a square of statues, and whispers followed us like fog.

"That's the one. That boy."

"Sure, he is."

"See the mark across the other one's eyes."

"Turn away from them. No, do not offer it."

Though every eye in the square was upon us, we both knew that we were absolutely alone. Everyone leaned away from us as if we were lepers, as if to touch us—even to speak with us—would infect them with the king's death sentence.

But still, there were the smells, and though I tried to keep my eyes away from an apple cart, I could not. When the farmer saw the hunger in my face, he turned away. I suppose he feared to give me—or even sell me—a single one of his windfalls.

"It is suddenly very quiet," said Innes.

"It is."

"Are we being stared at?"

"I suppose some dog somewhere in Wolverham is not looking at us."

"Does the dog have a bone he would share?"

I took his elbow, and we strode out across the square. But after a frozen night with little sleep and no food since yesterday noon, I could not take my eyes from the apples. The lovely, blushing, ruby red of the apples. I could hear the sharp sound of the bite, even taste the dry sweetness of it. I put my hand to my mouth as if holding one, and as soon as I let go of Innes, he crumpled.

How long had it been since *he* had last eaten?

"Innes!" I knelt down and slipped my hand under his head. "Innes, Innes," I whispered. "Innes!"

He smiled weakly. "Here."

"Innes, can you get up?"

"Tell the dog that I really would be grateful for the bone. I really would."

Then a shadow fell over us, dark and full, like a sudden eclipse. But when I looked up, there was no moon crossing the sun, but a face soft as a new leaf. It was a pudgy face, but the softness was not in that. And the cheeks did bulge some, but the softness was not in them either. It was in her eyes. And then she spoke, and it was in her voice too.

"By the good Saint Christopher himself, king or no king, I'll not let a child fall from hunger beside my own cart." She knelt beside me, soiling her cloak in the dirt of the slush, and with hands as big as shovels, she reached under Innes and lofted him close to her bosom. She peered down at him quietly, quietly; then she stood, hefting him as though he weighed nothing at all, as though she had carried him like this every day of her life. She turned, and I followed her to her covered cart and up three steps. Inside, she laid Innes down, gently, gently down, onto a cot and swaddled him with burlap.

"Wait here," she said to me, and went out and down the steps. I sat on the edge of the cot and felt Innes trembling beneath the covers.

She came back in just a moment, two steaming mugs in one hand. "Take one," she said to me, and as I drank it—tea and ale—she reached beneath Innes's head and lifted it. "A bit at a time. A bit. There. A little more. There."

The taste of it was spring sunshine, summer dew, fall frost. It was hard not to slosh it all down at once.

"You'll both be wanting some bread, would you, with sweet butter?" the woman asked.

"We'll be wanting it," Innes whispered.

"With some honey seeped in?"

"With honey seeped in," I answered.

When she handed half a loaf to me, I ate it all with hardly a breath between bites, the honey running down my cheeks and stickying my hands. Innes too ate quickly, his face always to the woman, as though he could watch her.

When we finished, she went outside with a bowl and returned with steaming water. She took a cloth and washed Innes's hands, then laid her own hand aside his head and guided it down onto the cot. Gently, gently she washed the wound across his forehead, dabbing at the dirt and dried blood until it shone pink and clean. Then she drew the burlap back, drew the rags of his shirt away, and washed the wounds across his chest, pulling away when he winced, returning even more gently.

And all the while she sang, a low, soft, swaying melody that set even the beating of my heart to its slow rhythm. I lay down on the floor beside the cot, the woman balled more burlap for a pillow, and I was asleep.

When I woke, Innes was still asleep. He had drawn his legs up almost to his chin and looked as if he could sleep through the Apocalypse. Still, the woman put her finger to her lips so I should not wake him, even if I could have. She sat at the back of the cart, stirring something in the crockery she held in her lap. It was a lap large enough for three, even four children to climb into.

I almost climbed in myself, wondering what it might be like.

She poured whatever she was stirring into a wooden bowl. "Here, then, eat this," she said, handing it to me. "It's hot," she warned, "just in from the kettle," but I spooned it steaming into my mouth. Oatmeal. It was oatmeal. And it was spiced with cinnamon. It burned at my tongue, but there was a pleasure in feeling the heat of it pour down into my chest.

The woman smiled broadly. "It's a joy watching you eat," she said. "A joy such as I haven't had for this many a year. By Saint Julian himself, it does me good."

"Has he left any for me?"—this from Innes, who hadn't been so deeply asleep that the smell of food would not wake him.

She poured some into another bowl and handed it to him. "It's quite—" but he had already taken a heap into his mouth.

He yelped, took in a great breath, and yelped again. "Hot," he said.

The woman reared back; I watched the laughter bubble and churn in her belly, flow upward to set the broad shoulders shaking, quiver into her neck, blow out her cheeks, and then spill out from her lips in a great cascade that filled the cart and set it rocking on its wheels.

"A burned tongue is hardly something to laugh at," complained Innes, blowing at his bowl.

"No," she answered when she could stop the cascade. "A burned tongue is hardly something to laugh at. But as Saint John of Saxony says—bless his holy name—when we laugh, we escape the Devil. And you'll notice that there's no Devil in here, though God knows there is more than one devil out and about in Wolverham this day."

"If there are devils about, they haven't brought their heat with them. We had a cold enough night of it."

"But this one had a warm enough afternoon yesterday, from what I hear tell," she said, pointing at me. "Is it true? Did you stand before the king and defy him?"

"I stood before the king, true enough."

"Well, then, you have the heart of Saint Catherine, and you shame us all who will not stand there with you. By the look of the welt across your face, the king did not take your boldness kindly."

"I don't believe he struck me because of that."

"Why, then?"

"Maybe he was afraid."

"Afraid of you?"

"Not of me."

She nodded knowingly. "Well, there is still the welt to care for anyway." From the pocket hanging at her belt she plucked a finger of herbs, their purple pale with drying. She crushed them in a bowl and poured in a thimble of water, and their scent filled the cart. "Would you flinch if I told you this will sting?"

"No."

"So." And gently, softly, she rubbed at the bruise, washing away the dry clots until clean blood showed, then stopping it with a cloth. Gently, softly, she rubbed the herb lotion into the wound. It did sting, and I did not flinch.

Then she sat on the cot beside Innes, drew me to her, held us both, and sang a sweet song to us, a song about the moon, about a faraway kingdom, about the sea. The words were waves that washed against us warmly.

"I may have heard that song once," Innes said quietly.

"No, no. You haven't. It's my own dear song, and I've sung it only to my babies."

"Where are your babies now?" asked Innes.

"Out into the wide world, who knows where, who knows how. If Saint Caedmon himself were to sing that song to them, there's not one of them who would remember. Well, perhaps one. But he has been gone this many a year, and there's no bringing him back."

"Which one?" asked Innes.

"Time was when I was the nurse living in the castle in the days of the old king, when the king that is now was ever so much smaller than you both. Before gold meant more to him than sunshine. I dandled him on my knee for a year, I did. And when the time came for him to marry and have his own son, I dandled that one as well. There was a baby who was a pleasure to tend. His laughter could cheer the whole of the castle. But it was a castle that no longer wanted cheering."

"I'm sorry," Innes said, but she was not looking at us anymore. She was looking out beyond the canvas of the cart, into another place. Then she shook her head as if to clear it.

"But that is all over now. No pining over that. And if I hadn't left the castle, then I never would have met my husband, would I? And him a sexton, no less."

"Mother," I asked, "if you were the king's own nurse, perhaps you could answer the riddle he set."

"Mother," whispered Innes. She turned to him. "Mother," he whispered again. She placed her hand against his cheek. It covered most of his face.

"I was never the clever one to answer riddles," she said. "And it's been too, too long, eleven years, since I was in his service. And he is not the child he was when I knew him."

"If we cannot answer the riddle," said Innes, "everyone who was arrested will die."

She stared at Innes, stared at him as the king had the day before. Then she waved her hand in the air, as if to brush aside sadness. "If it's the king's riddle you want answered, you might try the queen. But then you'd need to ride yourself to Eynsham and the abbey. Now there's a journey."

"Would you come with us to see her?" I asked, and the woman's face turned into a smile.

"To see the queen again. It's something I had never hoped to do. Poor dear, it's not the life she would have chosen. And as Saint Ethelred himself would say—"

But we did not discover what Saint Ethelred himself would say. Three soft raps struck the side of the cart. "You are discovered!" came a loud whisper. Immediately she quieted, put her finger to her lips, and moved forward to peer out. The sounds of the square had stilled, and when I saw her shoulders stiffen, I knew that there was a reason.

Until that moment I had never really known the kind of fear that freezes in the gut. Da had never let there be a moment when I could have been afraid. If I even whimpered in a dream, the lanterns in my room would spurt into a bright glow and the dying embers in the fireplace flare into brilliance. As for the battering thunder that came off the mountains, Da could call it out of a clear sky with a wave of a finger, and set folks down below us looking wonderingly at the blue sky. There had never been anything to fear.

But I was afraid now. My stomach tightened and my legs weakened. I hoped I wouldn't heave up the oatmeal.

"We did not laugh enough," the woman said. "Come see."

I peered out from the edge of the canvas. At first it seemed that nothing was unusual. Geese still squawked as buyers held them upside down, and pigs squealed in blood terror. But all the hawkers were still, almost every face in the square downturned. Except one. Half hidden behind a black hood, one face was moving around the square, looking behind barrels, under carts. He strode his brawny self cockily, and no one stood in his way. His mailed hand held the hilt of a short, stabbing sword tethered to his side.

The nurse pulled me back under the cover of the cart. "If there's laughter in you, now is the time to use it—but very quietly." Innes asked no questions. He sat still, waiting for the nurse to tell him—to tell us—what to do. She took Innes by the shoulder and stooped him beneath the cot, draping the burlap over the side so that it might cover him. Then she looked around to see what to do with me.

"Old woman," came a voice loud and sudden from the back of the cart. "Old woman, I am told that you entertain guests."

With a great shove of her hand she pushed me forward. I slipped out from the front canvas and across the seat, and leapt down between the harnessed horses, rubbing their sides to keep them from whinnying.

"Is it a law then that guests are not to be entertained?" she called.

The cart tilted back suddenly. "You. Nurse, you should not have returned to Wolverham."

"I am come to the market only."

"You are come to meddle, as you always did. Your meddling banished you from the castle. And almost worse, at my word."

"I have never doubted that it was at your word. But I am alone here, as you see."

"Those in the square say you were not alone."

"Those in the square are eager for rewards."

"And you are not."

"I am not." I heard the scraping of things moved about. "By Saint Ciaran himself, I tell you that you will find no one here with me."

"A saint whose name I have never heard."

"The wonder of it is that there is any saint whose name you have heard."

"Nurse," and here the voice came low. "Do not meddle again. Remember what I am called now." A jolting down the back steps of the cart. I hunched lower between the horses until I saw the nurse wave to me.

"Quickly," she whispered. I leapt inside and knelt by Innes beneath the cot. "That will be enough marketing for today." She clambered down the steps, then began to throw pots, tongs, and piles of turnips into the cart, finishing by swinging the steps up and tying them to. Then she climbed up the front and sat down heavily.

"Nurse," asked Innes, "what is his name?"

She bowed her head. "The King's Grip. He has no other name now. But by Saint Catherine he'll have no blood on his sword today."

"The king promised us seven days," I said. "Seven whole days."

"'The king promised,'" she snorted angrily. "'The king promised.' What this king promises and what he gives are fish and fowl. He must believe that you can solve the riddle and so sends his Grip to stop you." She turned back and looked at me, a smile pushing up her cheeks. "Tell me, are you always this offensive to royalty?"

"But I saw his eyes when he gave us the riddle. I don't believe that he does want to stop us."

"I have seen the results of the tasks he sets," she answered.

A sharp slap of reins, and we felt the first reluctant turn of the wheels, jerking over the cobblestones. I willed them to roll faster, faster, though I knew their clatter might attract the eye of the King's Grip.

More cobblestones rolled past, and more, the cart swaying back and forth, the wheels slipping some on the rounded stones. I thought of the soft pine-needle path that stretched through the woods, the sure steps of the Dapple. And then the wagon lurched to a halt, both horses whinnying. "By Saint Alban's eyes," the nurse bellowed, "you'd do well to lay your hand aside from that bridle."

"All carts leaving the square are to be searched, in the king's name."

"For criminal turnips?"

"For two young rebels. Step down."

"I'll not. I've been searched already once this morning, and I'll not stop for it again."

I heard the scraping of a sword being pulled from its scabbard. "This search is in the king's name, and there will be no asking again."

The nurse gave a long, long sigh. "So you'd see my turnips. Then come around back and I'll lower the steps." I shoved Innes beneath the cot again and scooted beside him; a burlap blanket was all that hid us, and capture meant ... What capture meant was not to be thought of. We pushed farther beneath the cot, back into the shadows.

But there was no need. With a sudden cry the nurse struck the horses to a gallop, and the wagon reeled back and forth, rolling us both from under the bunk. What with the battering of the cobblestones, the clanking of pans, and the overturning of a barrel of turnips, it seemed that Chaos itself had erupted all about us. A sudden iron clang, and four arrows puncturing through the canvas told us the guards at the city gates were not glad of our leave-taking.

"That last arrow," I yelled, "came just past your ear."

"They aim well," Innes shouted back. "Perhaps it would be best to keep low."

It would have been impossible to stand in any case. The cart was running smoother now that it had come out of the square and off the cobblestones, but the careening speed kept us both on the floor so that we would not be tossed through the canvas.

A sudden *thunk* as another arrow came through and bit into the wooden frame. Out the back flaps I saw three horsemen, two with bows. Another arrow came in, just over our heads.

"Those horsemen are holding on with just their legs," I called back to Innes.

"They must have horses that are not afraid of them. Do you think you could knock them off?"

"If I had something to throw."

He groped around, found a turnip, and handed it to me. "Throw it at the horses' heads," Innes said.

I took it from him and paused, weighing it in my hand. "I hardly want to throw one at a horse."

"Tousle," he said patiently, "those are not turnips coming our way."

I rose to my knees, steadied myself against the roll, and threw the first one. It smashed against the back frame of the cart.

"What luck?" Innes called.

"A near miss. I'll try another." And I did, and though I got it out of the cart, the turnip landed far off the mark.

Again and again I threw the turnips, Innes reaching about and then handing them to me one by one. And again and again they missed wildly as the arrows came thwacking in. Finally, half desperate, I threw as the cart leapt over a ridge in the road, and the turnip rolled and tumbled in the air until it met the tender tip of the front horse's snout. The effect was astonishing, and as I ducked an arrow that streamed in ferociously just above my shoulder, the horse jolted backward, reared up, and dropped its rider.

"Innes, the first one! The first one is down with one of your wicked turnips. Innes!"

But he did not answer. When I looked about, he was lying in the cart, his face as white as a cloud, his shoulder bright red with the blood spurting from an arrow shaft.

I turned back to the horses. I weighed a turnip, then threw it with all the hatred that had ever been behind the heft of any weapon. It smashed against the second horse's eye and turned him sideways, so the horse behind rushed into him with flailing hooves. Even the wild riding of the cart did not drown out their screaming.

Or mine.

chapter four

"Tousle!" The nurse was calling, her voice desperate. "Tousle, you need to come forward."

"Innes has an arrow in him, just above the shoulder."

"Come forward now," she called.

The nurse never turned away from the racing horses. Their breaths came in great snorts, and the white sweat that coated their bodies spattered back to us in gobs. "They're all done in with this. Listen to me." A ridge in the road lifted her nearly off the seat, and one of the horses stumbled. "Listen to me. Find the queen at Saint Eynsham Abbey and ask her the riddle. She'll know the answer, if anyone is to know it."

"You've got to stop for Innes," I called back.

"There's no help for him if we stop now," she screamed back at me. "Go back. Draw the arrow out, quick and sharp, and then press his hand to it."

"The three horses are down."

"By Saint Brendan, it's not the horsemen we're to worry about. Now, you've got to pull the arrow out. And straight, with no twist at all to it, and no up and down."

"But I never—"

"Do it now. And by Saint Margaret, pull it straight."

I went back to Innes and looked at the blood and sweat on his chest.

"You're to pull it out," he said.

"I am."

"Then do it," he said.

I nodded. I grabbed the arrow with both hands.

"Do it!" Innes cried, and I jerked it out from him, and jerked out a cry from his throat as well, and a fountain of blood from the wound. Quickly I held his hand to the spurting, then tore off a long strip of the burlap and wrapped it around him, all the time blood running down. So much blood running down. Innes's skin was the yellow-white of old clouds.

"Is it done?" called the nurse, looking back. "Then settle him onto the cot, with his shoulders high. No, higher."

Innes groaned with my fussing and with the charging of the cart across ruts that seemed as large as ditches. I changed the burlap strips again and again, but the red stains sprouted across them like impossible blossoms, and I pressed my hands against them to hold the life inside.

"Is he still bleeding, then?" cried the nurse.

"Still bleeding."

"And if you hold your hands against the bandage?"

"It still bleeds through."

With a rough pull the nurse hauled back on the reins, hefting the horses back into a trot, then a snorting walk, their heads whisking about to toss the lather from their mouths. "Take the reins," she called to me.

"I've never driven a cart before."

"Neither of the horses will know that. Keep them to a walk. If they want to take their head, pull them like so. Just so." She handed the reins to me and went back to Innes. "And as Saint Leoba says, 'Let the eyes of the unjust be blind.'"

After the rush and speed of the wagon, the gait now seemed horribly slow, and I kept turning my head to see if pursuit had caught us. The nurse bent hugely over Innes, crushing so many green herbs into his wound that the scent of damp moss filled the air. She sang her low lullaby as she worked, and it seemed to me—though this must have been impossible—that she was suddenly happy. Her face had taken on a kind of straight and efficient smile, her lips opening at the words of the song, then closing as the song descended to a hum. Her rubbing hand moved in time to its rhythms.

"The bleeding has stopped," she soon called to me softly. "But it would take only a rock against a wheel to start it again. He's got to be still for the wound to close. And this cart is not the place for a body to be still."

"It is also the very thing that the king's soldiers will be looking for."

She nodded slowly. "Not far away, on the river side of the road, there is an old mill."

"I passed it just yesterday morning."

"Well," she said, "I have known the miller there and his wife. It would be a place to hide Innes until the wound closes. Or at least for the night."

"I passed the mill yesterday morning just by chance," I said, half in a whisper.

"Nothing is ever quite by chance. Go along now. And keep the gait slow. Mind the black horse most especially."

Nothing is ever quite by chance.

I minded the black horse most especially, but he was too tired from his run to cause mischief. We plodded along slowly, while everything in me wanted to whip the horses to a gallop. Slowly the houses started to spread themselves out, slowly the gardens and fields grew larger, and slowly, slowly the mill finally slouched into view. From this side the mill seemed to lean out over the water, its wheel about to tilt in.

"There," the nurse called. "Stop just there."

"The house is on the far side."

"There are reasons for not telling the miller and his wife that you are here. Now help me. I'll see that the wound is fair and clear and then be off with the cart."

"It would be warmer in the house."

"Warmer than you'd like, if the King's Grip comes."

"No reason for him to stop here, of all places."

"Reason enough. Now," she said, gesturing, "there will be bandages there, and two blankets just there. No, by your other hand. Bring them along. And that pouch of herbs there too. And you might as well bring the rest of the oatmeal, if the crockery is not all smashed." While I gathered everything up, she reached under Innes and tucked him to her, all the while crooning her soft lullaby.

The sunlight glinted off the rimy stones of the mill as we carried Innes across, keeping ourselves out of sight of the house beyond. The wheel creaked slowly about as if it were hardly aware of what it was doing. Water sloshed lazily from its troughs and ran over the icy coating that the winter had built up along its edges. Inside, it was warmer but dark as dark. The mill's innards groaned with the crabbed turning of the wheel outside, almost as if it were groaning with Innes. I waited for my eyes to pick out shapes and found myself rubbing the grain dust away from them. It filled the air so thickly, I wondered for a moment if I could drown in it.

"The stairs are there," the nurse called, and we climbed them to the thrumming of the mill wheel. The floors, the beams that spanned overhead, the very air vibrated with the turning. Up in the loft a slit of a window let in enough light to see sacks of properly stacked meal. I pulled three from the pile and spread them flat, then laid a blanket over them all. The nurse laid Innes down and checked the bandage, fussing at its tightness but glad that no new blood showed.

I huddled back against the roughness of the sacks while she fussed, and the smell of the meal dusted up. I closed my eyes and was at once home again with Da, each of our hands yellow with the meal of the week's baking. The smell of the fire, the lumps of dough rolling themselves out to rise, the taste of the meal in the air—they were all so sharp that I almost reached forward for them.

"I'll be going now and leaving you to Saint Jude of blessed memory," said the nurse. She had to yell against the thrumming.

I knew she would have to go. She would hurry the cart along and drag with it any searching horsemen, like wood chips in a boat's wake. Only this time if the Grip caught her, he would not simply warn her against meddling. I nodded as she pointed to the bandages. "A change at nightfall, and again in the morning. As gentle as ever you can." I nodded again, and she took my face in her huge hands, leaned forward, and pressed her forehead against mine, her nose against mine. Then she reached down and scooped the thick meal dust into her hands. "Let the eyes of the unjust be blind," she said again. She started down the ladder, looked at us once more, and was gone. I was left with the thrumming and with Innes.

I had never been kissed so before. The newness of it and the loss of it were all mixed up together, and I could say nothing in the heat of that mix.

Sitting there, I thought it seemed that this was all one of Da's phantasms. In a moment he would shake his hands and the air would swirl and the misty pictures dissolve. We would pick up our mugs and laugh and stretch our feet out to the fire. But it was no phantasm. The thrumming of the mill wheel and the labor of Innes's breathing were both real.

We slept. Warm and tight against the sacks, we slept.

When I opened my eyes, it was still light, the kind of light that lies low on the land late on a winter afternoon. Innes was still asleep, his breathing less harsh now. Nothing else moved. All was absolutely quiet. But something had wakened me.

Then I knew: It was the quiet that had wakened me. The mill wheel had stopped.

I crawled to the edge of the loft stairs and peered down at the very moment that the miller was thrust into the mill by the King's Grip, the miller's wife following closely behind. With mailed hands the Grip pulled the miller's smock and lifted him up, holding him so close that it seemed as if he were about to bite him. The miller's wife stood still, her hands smothered in her apron, afraid to plead with anything but her eyes.

With a jerk the Grip tossed the miller into a heap, and his wife immediately rushed over and knelt between them. But the Grip ignored them. Instead, he drew his sword and began to poke it into the sacks, one after another, until he walked ankle deep in the meal that poured from them. The miller and his wife stayed on the floor, watching.

I had seen battles in the conjurings that Da had set in the air before us. I had seen the murderous rage in the eyes of the great Achilles as he stalked Hector, then slew him with a sweeping stab. I had never understood the blood lust that reddened his face. I did now.

The Grip sauntered to the staircase and set his foot on the first step. I scuttled back, crossed the floor, leapt over the sacks, and huddled quietly beside Innes. I wished that the thrumming would cover us again.

"Master," I heard the miller call, "no one has been up those stairs these five days and more. You see yourself that the dust lies thick upon them."

I waited, my breath like a millstone in my chest. The first step creaked under the weight of the Grip.

"With a simple push," the Grip said, "I could split this beam and bring this mill to a ruin. Two, maybe three more winters will bring it down for me. How is it, miller, that fortune changes so quickly for some? You, who might have been miller to the king himself, as wealthy and envied as any merchant has ever been."

"On the darkest days," said the miller wearily, "I think it but chance."

"Chance or design, you have lost everything on a boast."

"Not everything," said the miller's wife.

As I listened to their voices coming up through the floorboards, I imagined her taking her husband's hand in her own and fronting this man with the short sword.

A long pause, with some scuttling below. Then the Grip's voice came again. "Chance or design, the end is the same. But here is my design: See to it that you do all as I told you.

The reward is large should you be the one to find them. The penalty for hiding them is even larger. And the king is of a mind that no one—not even those closely connected—will be spared his anger. Now bring some bread. And I'll take that bottle, and that. Load them into the saddlebags quickly and hope that I decide not to take anything else. Your ear, or perhaps her nose."

I heard a bustle below, then the grating sounds of the Grip's footsteps, a whistle and the sharp snort of the horse, and, after a moment, a gallop. I sank back against the meal sacks. "What fills a hand fuller than a skein of gold?" I wondered, and held my own hand up to look at it. I could barely make it out in the wasted light. What might fill my hand? I let it drift to my forehead to touch the spot where the nurse had touched me.

The sound of someone slowly ascending the stairs. A pause. I backed against the sacks, making myself as small as ever I could. Then a whisper filtered up through the dust like a distant memory.

"You needn't be afraid now." I peered out from behind the meal at the miller's wife, who stood with open hands looking into the loft. "It's all right. The miller will watch a moment against his return, but he is sure to be off to burn some barn or smash the windows of a manor house or two. That's the way of it with his type."

I stood up, wonderingly. "You knew we were here all along?"

"Not until the King's Grip started up the stairs. We saw the meal dust fall through the flooring as you ran across. He saw it too, but he didn't know what it meant; fancy that. There's to be some good in working a mill all your life long." She crossed the loft and stood over us. "You're the boy from yesterday," she said, and I nodded.

When she saw Innes, she looked at him with an almost aching tenderness. She went to the top of the stairs and called the miller, who came with hands roughened by his work to pick up Innes as easily as a sack of flour. He balanced him down the loft stairs and out the mill with his wife mothering behind him.

"You're not to sling him about like your grain," she scolded. "And you'll be watching his head by the doorway. No, his head, you numb miller."

The miller nodded patiently.

"Mind you lay him gently on the cot. Gently. Is that gently?"

I followed behind, hoping that the miller would not open the shoulder wound more. As it was, the bandage was tinged red. But the miller held Innes like a wounded lamb and laid him down like a baby into feathers. He did not groan.

"Now take your chunky self away and let me tend to him," the miller's wife said, and he turned to me and shrugged his shoulders, a look of exasperated and long-suffering love on his face.

"There's not a thing to do with her when she's like this but to stumble along behind the millstone."

He was a short, thick man, but short as he was, he could have touched the ceiling of the cottage. Its roof squatted down to him, its center beam bowing and one corner sagging like a man in a stupor. The chimney stones stomached out, two iron braces angling against their collapse. It was a house that had settled into itself.

While the miller's wife fussed over Innes, clucking at the wound, and while the miller bustled through the house to find the new shirt his wife was calling for, I stood by the trestle table and smelled. Just smelled. It was filled with loaves of braided bread, bread speckled with cinnamon, bread yellow with its cheesy crusting, bread filled with the last of the fall apples.

"The boy looks hungry, my dear. It's a glory you've done the baking, or he might wither away as he stands in front of us." The miller laughed deep and low.

"When we laugh, we escape the Devil," I said automatically, and was startled to see how they both turned toward me, open-mouthed.

"There's been many a turning of the mill wheel since last I heard that," said the miller slowly.

"I heard it myself just today," I answered, "but . . ." And I looked longingly at the table.

With a smile the miller brought me close to the fire, laid a wooden trencher in my lap, and ladled in stew.

Stew! How could I have missed its meaty bubbling? When he ladled it out, the steam curled into the room. I shoveled it into my mouth, finishing the bowl before the miller had torn a hunk of bread for me.

"Is he about to start on the furniture, or has he left some stew for me?" said Innes, rising on an elbow.

"Should someone wounded be eating?" I asked.

"Should someone wounded be eating!" he yelled back.

"Though it was just a nick, hardly anything to talk about at all."

"Hardly anything to talk about?"

"At all."

Innes sighed deeply. "Daggers, arrows, horses. And now to die of starvation, when the food is so close by that I can smell it."

"Then here," I said, and I filled my own trencher up and sat beside him on the bed, holding the bowl for him as he spooned the meaty stuff into his mouth, feeding himself so quickly that he almost forgot to breathe, and gasping at the pleasure of the taste.

The miller and his wife stood by the fire quietly, hand in hand, watching us both. They fitted into each other, as if the curves and bumps of their bodies had grown accustomed. They stared at us, stared as though amazed. "He's so like," she said. "The way he holds his head, the way he speaks, the corners of his smiles. They are all the same."

But the miller shook his head. "We've hoped a thousand times, and a thousand times learned the better of it."

"But this one time."

"No, wife. No. Now, these are the boys the Grip wants, and they'll be needing to get away. And no later than morning." He turned to us. "He'll watch at the main road, so you'll need another way. A fistful of gold and we'd put an ocean between you and the king, but there is none to be had here."

"If we had the gift of it, we could spin some out," I said.

The miller and his wife stared at me.

"Spin some out?" he said.

"Yes, spin some out. Da does it often enough, just for the pleasure of the spinning. Afterward we leave it outside for the birds."

The miller and his wife were very still. Then, slowly, the miller's wife reached out her hand and touched my shoulder. Her eyes welled. "Boy, what is your name?"

"Tousle."

She turned back to Innes, then to me, then back to Innes again, her hands up to her face. "He is so like ..." she said to herself again, and paused as the miller took her hand in his.

"No, wife. The water has flowed too far and too long, and it does not flow upstream again."

"How many times have you heard of a man who can spin straw into gold?" she asked, then turned again to me. "Your mother. Tell us about her."

"I never knew her."

"You know nothing about her?"

"Nothing."

"And you," she asked, turning to Innes. "What of your mother?"

Innes spread his hands wide and said nothing.

"You too know nothing about her? Not a thing? Isn't there some small part of her that stays with you?"

"Nothing," said Innes. It was the emptiest word I had ever heard.

"And your father?" she asked, turning back to me eagerly, leaning forward, holding hard to my hand now.

"Da? Da is Da."

"Are you much like him? The look of you, I mean."

"No. Not at all."

At this the miller's wife stepped back and again put her hand to her mouth. She turned again from me to Innes, then back again.

"Wife, this cannot be. He is long dead." But she only shook her head and watched me, unblinkingly. "Wife, even if it was him, he still must be away. Perhaps even tonight. Perhaps in the hay cart."

"If we were to be found in your hay cart, the king would hear of it," said Innes.

"Then the king would hear of it," answered the miller gruffly. "There is no cause to love the king in this house. And there is great cause to help those who will not bow the knee to his whims, as I once did."

"The king set us a riddle," I said. "A riddle we need to answer within the next six days."

The miller nodded. "The king was ever a lover of riddling."

I wondered how it was that a miller would know this, but I did not ask. "If we can solve it, he will free all the prisoners he has condemned."

"His promises are always vast," said the miller's wife. "Tell us the riddle."

"What fills a hand fuller than a skein of gold?"

"Two skeins," the miller said immediately. "The answer is two skeins. More than anything else, the king has always wanted gold. And if he had one skein of gold in his hands, it would bring him no pleasure unless he might have two."

"You are sure of this?" asked Innes.

The miller nodded. "I learned it too late, and to my own sorrow. But what good will even the answer do you? If you solve the riddle, do you think he will clap you merrily on the back and send you off with prisoners dancing behind you? He will not even let you approach before he cuts you down."

"He made the promise before the Great Lords."

But the miller gave only a bitter laugh. "A skein of gold for each prisoner might bring release. But nothing else will—most especially a promise."

"First the answer," said Innes. "Then we shall see what comes with the day."

A short, guttural sob from the miller's wife, and she turned to her husband and held him.

Through the windows I watched the sky cloaking into dark. The last light lit the undersides of bulbous clouds waddling in, heavy with their snow. Already the night air was seeping beneath the cottage door and winding its way around my feet.

"It's to be a cold night," said the miller. "If we're to have these boys gone beyond easy reach by morning, we'll need to be leaving."

She looked at him, then smiled. "You never did find that shirt, or another for Tousle," she said, wiping at her eyes. "Leave it to me, and you find a sack we might fill for them. Go on, now. Yes, yes, go on." Then slowly, hardly taking her eyes from us, she climbed the steep stairs into the loft.

"I'd best be taking the bow," called the miller after her.

She leaned down from the loft. "You haven't strung that bow for more years than you or I can count."

"Well," he said, taking a bow and quiver from a nail beneath the stair overhang, "that hardly matters. Not a single one of these arrows has a head."

"Then what earthly good will it do to take it?"

He shrugged his shoulders and smiled at us as he slung the quiver over his shoulder. "You won't be long up there?"

"Long enough to find the shirts you could not."

She was long up there, but when she came down, she brought with her two fine woven shirts. She handed one to me, then turned to Innes and helped him change. I stripped off my own shirt—I was almost as bloody as Innes—and was about to put on this new one when I heard the miller gasp.

At the same moment, the door smashed open. With a single long stride the Grip strode in and twisted my arm behind my back. Quickly, expertly, he unsheathed his sword and held it tight against my throat.

"Meal through the floorboards," he said quietly, and smiled.

chapter five

The cold line pressed against my throat, but it was nothing to the fire in my shoulder with my arm twisted and held high behind my back.

"Master," came the controlled and slow voice of the miller, "I'm known in these parts as one who never misses his aim."

"The same is said of me," replied the Grip, and he grinned.

"Then you know that should you even prick that boy, I'll have an arrow into you before you see blood."

The Grip laughed. "He'll be dead and I'll be at your throat before you fit an arrow to the bow."

"Master, folks hereabouts live by poaching, and being that a poacher hunts at the same time he himself is hunted, his hands are faster than fast, and his aim surer than sure. You'll never see the arrow drawn from the quiver and fitted, any more than the doe that ends up on this table, and she with eyes sharper than yours might ever hope to be."

The Grip held still.

"I'd pay good and close heed to him, Master," said Innes. "I've never seen him come close to missing."

"Boy," growled the Grip, "I'm here for this one. But no one will squawk if I let your blood as well."

"No," replied Innes, his voice low. "No one would." Even with the sword at my throat I was startled by the bitterness in his voice.

"But you would have another soul heaped on your back," said the miller's wife. She stepped to Innes and drew his head against her.

"An easy load to bear," snarled the Grip.

The miller drew a hand up to one of the arrow shafts. "By all that's holy, I can sink a shaft through an eye before you blink. Take your hands away from the boy."

The Grip hesitated and then took the sword from my neck. He let go my arm and it dangled down, the fire so sharp I could hardly keep from crying out.

"Tousle," said the miller. I looked down toward the blade, then slowly started backward away from it. Beads of sweat ran down my sides, and my breathing was short. I still clutched the shirt in my hand.

The Grip straightened, holding the sword in front of him. He balanced it in his hand, then sheathed it. "Miller, it makes no difference if I take him here, now, or if I take him in a day or two. None to me, at least. For that matter we can stay here and play the game out until six more suns have set. But, miller, the boy will never finish his business with the king, my life upon it."

"Yes," said the miller, "your life upon it."

The Grip's mouth worked back and forth, and the hand holding the sword hilt grew white-knuckled. Then he exploded. "Do you know what it is to feel the rage of the

Great Lords? And what is this boy to you? Nothing. I could take him now and be about my business. We'll be gone and all will be as it was before."

"No," said the miller's wife.

"No," said the miller.

"You've played the fool all your life, and now you play it again. By all that's holy, you never had to send your daughter to Wolverham. The thing was a wisp of the king's fancy, a whim at the end of a hunt. He would have forgotten come morning, and you none the worse for your silly boast."

"He would not have forgotten the spinning of gold."

"He would have forgotten. He is the creature of a moment. All that happened, miller, happened at your designing, and you see now the end. Design again and protect this boy, and I will burn this house, and your mill, around your ears. There is no jest here, miller. I will fill my hands with the ashes of your mill."

"Tousle," said the miller. "You hear the choice. I could send you with the King's Grip, or I could keep you from him." The miller's hand reached out and gripped his wife's shoulder. "We have had this choice before," he said to her, and she nodded. Then he turned to me. "If there is design in this, remember what I choose to do this time. Run, Tousle. Run, Innes. Run and do not look back. And this Grip and I will be about our business."

I dropped the shirt over my head. The miller's wife looked at us, and she smiled. Tears wet the creases in her cheeks. "Go," she breathed, and she said it with a sigh, as if she had been waiting to say it for years. "Go, and God go with you."

I crossed to Innes and took him by the sleeve. Together we walked backward out the door and into the frosted night.

But we did not run.

The Grip's black horse, darker than the shadows, stood tied to a low hemlock. He was bigger by far than the Dapple or the Gray, and his steamy breath snorted up like a dragon's. I held Innes to a stop, then stepped to the horse slowly, one hand reaching out. He pulled at his reins, whinnying and tossing his head. If he hadn't been tied by the halter, he would have reared.

And suddenly I was back at Da's farm, the morning the Gray had first trotted out of the forest. Big eyed and blood flecked from ferocious spurs, he had galloped back and forth in the clearing, desperate and terrified, while I watched from the window. Then Da had gone out. Little Da, so tiny against the rearing horse. With one hand outstretched, he had walked steadily, clucking softly, until the horse calmed and stood, eyes still big, still watching. Da had stood on his toes and reached up until the horse leaned his head down. When Da first touched him, the Gray's sides flicked out with fear, but he did not move. He whinnied once, but by the time Da had begun to stroke his neck, the Gray had stuck his muzzle in Da's jerkin. I was not at all surprised when he pulled out a block of sugar.

"Quiet," I told Innes. "If I move slowly enough, he'll stay calm and we can ride him. Otherwise he'll bolt."

Innes nodded his head. "A horse a breath away from me will bolt if I do not stay quiet. And probably he will bolt right over me."

"Yes."

"I'll stay quiet."

"Shh ..." I hushed, waving at Innes with my hand, then realizing that that would not be much help. I moved closer to the horse, who watched my outstretched arm suspiciously with big, white eyes. He tried to rear again. Slowly, clucking my tongue, wishing I had a block of sugar, I reached out to stroke him but pulled back when the horse whinnied shrilly. I reached again and saw the sides of the horse's mouth being ripped by the bit. A surge of anger, and I grabbed at the halter, fumbling at the bridle until it gave. A scream from the horse, and I ducked under the head and unbuckled the other side. Then, with a sudden jerk, he pulled his head out of the halter.

"There!" I cried, triumphant.

And he galloped off into the night, the sound of his hooves pounding the hardened road.

I stood holding the empty halter, wondering why I had been so foolish, and knowing why. I threw the halter into the wood. "At least the Grip will have no horse," I said.

"I told you they were afraid of me."

"Is the Grip afraid of you too?"

"Terrified," said Innes.

Even so, we ran in the cold night, Innes just behind me to follow the sound of my footsteps. We ran wildly until the frosty air burned our lungs. We slowed to a walk, then ran again as fear caught up to us. Through the night darkness we ran, the fear deep in our guts and the darkness thick around us. We ran as the moon hefted herself up into the tree branches, tangled for a bit, and then floated free in the sky, brightening the road to a shadowy white and making the woods along the roadside seem even darker. I kept the road fixed in my eye, wondering if I could ever find the path that led home, wondering if the trees would still stand apart.

And suddenly I realized that I was smiling, that I was

almost laughing. Da would have said I was a lunatic, but it wasn't that at all. The world was suddenly large and thrilling. Thrilling!

Farther and farther we ran. The moon reached her height and started to sink back down to the trees, and still we ran. The topmost branches caught her and began to drag her in, and still we ran. Only when her light was almost hidden by the trees did I know that I had missed the path home. Or that the path had closed in again and was not to be found.

I tried to crush down the panic that started to rise. A different thrilling.

"Tousle," panted Innes, stumbling to a halt. "Tousle, I can run for a while yet, but not a long while. Are we close?"

"No. I don't know."

A long pause.

"Well, then, it will be up to me to find a hiding place. How about if we start—"

"Innes, I'll find the place. I suppose we are easy to spot here in the middle of the road."

"Easy enough."

"So we should get off into the woods."

"The deeper the better."

"We might be easy to track in the woods. Here on the road the snow is all trampled."

"Then we must find a stream," said Innes, beating his sweaty sides against the cold.

"We cannot swim in freezing water."

"No," he answered, "but we can walk on ice and leave no tracks."

So on we ran, stopping now and again to listen for the sound of water, hoping that we would not hear the sound of pursuit.

Not long before morning we did finally come to a ford, though I might easily have missed it if the moon had not been showing her last light. There was no sound of the water—the river was a glass highway. Just as the stars were showing a little less fiercely to the east, I stepped onto it—and immediately I was on my back, my head rapping against the ice.

"Slippery?" asked Innes.

"No. Not at all. Just jump right on out."

So he did, and landed with his feet sure and his knees bent. He gave a push with his back foot and slid on past me. He twirled once, then again, and took a deep bow.

"Innes, where did you learn to do that?"

"A blind boy will learn anything to amuse a crowd and earn a loaf of bread. Anything."

"Innes," I said, "whatever happens after this, I promise that you will never have to amuse a crowd again." It was too dark to see his face fully. I hoped that he believed me, but I could not tell.

"You start," he said finally, "by setting the one foot across your body, like this. Keep the other pointed, then push off."

I got to my knees, then stood gingerly, watching him. "I suppose we should head east. We'll be harder to follow if someone is looking directly into the sun."

"And is Eynsham to the east?"

"That we will need to find as we go. Let me hold you." My hand in his, I crossed, pointed, and pushed.

"Now shove out to the sides," he called, and I followed stiffly, shuffling along the surface of the river, trying to ignore the thin, numbing film of icy water.

I grew accustomed to the gait, and we began longer shuffles. Usually we skirted the black rocks that thrust up through the ice, and only once we went over the darker ice that started to shatter with our weight. But all told we began to move quickly, though neither of us knew yet where it was we were headed.

The sky purpled. Holding one hand out for balance, I watched the grand show I had seen so often before, though now I kept looking behind as well for any pursuit. But in the yellowing air I heard only wakening birds, and soon the river bent and bent again, and I saw the world turn itself under and the sun heft over the horizon, startling the river to a white so bright that I had to shield my eyes as we skidded along. The sun rose up directly ahead, so big it might roll down the river toward us.

"Listen," said Innes suddenly.

I stopped, crouched down to make myself smaller, and looked behind us. Nothing. I expected to hear galloping horses, or shouts. Nothing but the morning birds.

"We'd best get off the ice," I said.

"No. Listen."

I strained my frosted ears.

"There. It's ended now."

"What's ended?"

Innes held his hands out, as though he were going to explain something to someone who most likely wouldn't understand. "The dawn. I've always been able to hear it. It's God's gift that's all my own, that's no one else's."

"You hear the dawn?"

"It starts low, almost so quiet that you're not really sure you hear it at all. Then there's a single bell, then another, and then it's all pealing like the bells of heaven are ringing with newness, pealing like no bells you've ever heard, Tousle. God Almighty, the dawn gives reason to hope."

I stared at Innes's enraptured face. "You must wish you could see it," I said.

"You must wish you could hear it."

I did. But I wished something else too. I wished I knew if there was a gift that was all my own.

Then suddenly I was back in another late-winter dawning, walking back with Da from the barn, a bucket brimming with milk in each straining hand. The dust of sweet hay lay in our noses, and as the sun struck us full on our backs and tossed our shadows toward the house, I smelled breakfast heating by the fire. The smell was so real, so very real, that sudden hunger overwhelmed me, and I wondered where in all this waste we might find food.

Innes held his face up to the air. "Tousle, are we near a cottage?"

"No. There's nothing."

"I smell bread baking."

"There's no bread baking. There's no fire for . . ." I paused at the sight of smoke curling over the trees on the far bank.

"So you smell it too?"

I did. Impossible as it was, the smell of baking bread wafted into the air. We both felt ourselves drawn toward it. We shuffled to the riverside, scrambled over ice-flecked rounded stones, and pushed through a thick grove of quiet aspens that hid a clearing from the river. The sun had just risen above the trees and was dropping light into the grove in great warm beams, light so warm that it was melting snow off the aspen branches and onto the shingled roof of a small cottage, tidy and perfect.

I had never seen it, but I knew right away that Da had conjured it. The sharp slant of the roof, the filigreed cornices, the carved wood of the door, the slight twist in the bricks of the chimney, all were smaller twins of the house where we lived—where I had lived. Even the color of the smoke, a sort of blue haze that paled to whiteness in spots, bespoke Da. And the smell of the bread—I had smelled it a hundred, a thousand times of a morning, and I knew it was Da's.

Dragging Innes with me, I burst open the door and stooped Innes through. The table was set with crockery, and the merriest fire in all the world leapt up suddenly to greet us. Bread stood and waited on warming bricks, guarded by a thick jug of steaming cider whose handle plucked out its cork when we came in. "Da," I called. But there was no answer. I went back to the door and called out in the clearing. Still no answer. But he had been here. He had been here.

The bread was still warm to the touch and steamed when I broke it open. And the cider! The sweet cider! I felt its heat spread through my chest and down into my guts. We drank and drank again, and ate without talking, without thinking of anything but the heady taste of it all.

That bread filled me with new hope, like Innes's dawn. If we could find bread and sweet cider by a riverside in late winter, then why should we not find the answer to the riddle and bring it to Wolverham? And perhaps we had the answer already.

"Innes," I asked, "do you think the miller was right? That the answer to the riddle is another skein of gold?"

Innes shrugged his shoulders. "It seems too easy an answer. It's such a strange riddle that there must be more to it than simply another skein."

I nodded slowly, remembering the king's eyes. "Yes," I agreed, "it is too easy."

Filled and warm, we stretched out, our heads by the fire.

I felt Da all around me. I could almost hear him, almost smell him. I checked the bandage that crossed Innes's chest, then followed him into sleep. If the Grip had ridden his horse right into the cottage, I would have slept on still.

When I woke, Innes was up and sitting by the fire, and I watched him a moment, moving as he did in a world that was always dark. I stretched out, folded my arms behind my head, and yawned.

"You're awake."

"Innes," I asked, "do you think about it often, being blind?"

He shrugged. "There are days when I do. It might almost have been better if I had never seen. Then seeing and not seeing would all be one to me. But I do remember seeing." He stretched his hand out. "I remember firelight. I remember the sky, the sun. I remember one stunted little tree I would put my arms around. I remember my own hand."

"That's not very much."

"No, not much."

"Do you remember how . . ."

He nodded. "I heard the story often enough afterward. This is not the first time a village has rebelled against Lord Beryn. The last time, he chose my family as the example in the village." Innes paused, his mouth open as if to howl, working back and forth as though the howl could not get out. "They held me to watch what they did to my father, my mother. And then Lord Beryn turned his sword at me. 'This one will be my living memorial to all who would rebel,' he said."

Innes shook his head. "Do you know, Tousle, every time people in the village saw me, they remembered what Lord Beryn had said. And they pitied me, then hated me for making them remember."

"So no one took you in."

"For a time they did. First one family, then another. But it was a poor village. And after all, there is no place in this wide world for a boy with no parents, no eyes. Whom can he apprentice to? What trade can he carry? What learning can he perform? Leave him to tend the horses. And if he cannot do that, send him to another house to feed. He can saw wood. And if he cannot do that, to another house. He can muck out the barn. And if he cannot do that . . . if he cannot do even that, then play the fool with him and throw him a crust of bread for the pleasure it brings to you."

He stilled, and we let the silence speak between us. It spoke of years of loneliness.

"There wasn't anyone . . ."

"Not with these eyes. And if Lord Beryn were to return, who knew what might happen to the ones who took me in. In all that village there were just two girls, younger than me, who cared whether I lived through the night or not. And now they sit in chains back in Wolverham." He paused a long time. "They would bring me potatoes."

"And, Innes, we'll bring them the answer to the riddle. We'll find the way to Saint Eynsham Abbey. We'll find the queen and hear her answer to the riddle. And we'll bring it back to Wolverham."

A high, shrill whinny froze the air around us. The house seemed to shudder. The fire died to a glow, the shutters smacked tight against the windows, and the rafters hunched down over us.

"Perhaps," whispered Innes, "we should not be asking whoever is on that horse the way to Saint Eynsham Abbey."

"No, but we should be sure about who it is." Out the door, through the trees, and to the river, whose ice still shone bright white in the high sun. I peered past the aspens. There, picking his way carefully along the ice, placing each foot with exquisite care, a black horse came along, the clop of his hooves as they hit the ice unnaturally loud. The rider was hooded, sitting huge and dark in the saddle. "Is it possible that he can track over the ice?" I wondered, but then, with a sudden thought, I looked behind me and saw the blue smoke rising into the air.

A headlong rush back to the clearing. "Innes, Innes," I shouted in a whisper.

"Go," he called back. "He's looking for you, not me. Follow the river until you find someplace to hide."

I grabbed him by the elbow. "Stay close and keep a hand in front of your face," and together we ran from the hut and crashed through the woods, running now in blind panic, not thinking about the trampled snow and broken branches that proclaimed our passing to the world. Before long, twigs had whipped at both our faces and added blood to the trail.

"We have to stay by the river," Innes called. "That's where we'll find someone who knows of the Abbey."

"The Grip is tracking us by the river."

"No, wait," Innes said. I paused, my chest heaving. "He couldn't possibly follow us across the ice. Not even the Grip could do that. He must have guessed which direction we would take."

I nodded. "We're not the only ones who know that the queen might have the answer to the riddle."

"And we're not the only ones who know that the queen lives in Saint Eynsham Abbey."

"So he knew we would go there before we knew it ourselves."

"He knew," Innes agreed, and at my groan, he reached

out for my shoulder. "You do have to admire his skills," he said.

"Let's work our way back to the river," I said, then stopped. Behind us, billows of the blackest smoke rushed into the air, seething and boiling into the cold blue. "Da's cottage," I said half aloud.

"Burning," Innes said. "I can smell it."

I watched for a time as the smoke lobbed higher and higher and then was blown into long, dirty wisps by the wind. "This way," I said.

Long through that day, long past the time when we could still feel the warmth of the bread and cider in our guts, we fought our way through woods thicker than any I had ever seen, even in Da's phantasms. We went slower now, and wherever we could, we crossed granite outcroppings, changed our angles, used the ice of every tiny stream—anything to fool the Grip. We hardly spoke. We thought of nothing but reaching the river that seemed to curl always away from us. I began to wonder if there had ever been a time when we were not struggling past trees that stretched their jagged branches to swipe across our faces.

An hour before sunset—the end of the second day since we had heard the riddle—we found the river again. The water was open here, squeezed by close banks into a rush of white and dashing against its stone shores so loudly that we had to shout at each other. The mist thrown up by the rushing water soaked our faces and soothed our scratches. It had coated every tree with ice, and the trunks reached to the sky in white columns, holding up a canopy of gilded branches to the sunset.

The water thrummed, thrummed against the bedrock of the river, sending its heady vibrations up into the living stones and then into us; our muscles tingled with it. The sounds surrounded us like mountains. The huge, white, humpy river flowed with silky, quick ease, and who knew for how long it had been doing that, running day after day, unmoved by a hunt—or by a flight.

The banks were too steep to climb, and there was no ice to walk on here, so we followed the high banks along the river as dusk shadowed into the trees. And just when it was too dark to see the branches ahead of us, I saw the warm light of hearth fires through windows and knew that we had come to a village, perhaps Saint Eynsham itself.

chapter six

The lights of the village lay below us like blowzy stars. They flickered redly and now and again blinked when someone paused in front of them. Peaty smoke hovered in patches, scenting the air for a moment, then disappearing, then scenting it again as we came closer. All was as quiet as the dark: a startled cackle now and again from a hen suddenly awakened, two dogs baying back and forth at each other, a shutter slammed to—that was all the peaty air carried to us.

I felt again a secret thrill, coming up on a darkened village to discover the answer to a riddle, an assassin at our heels, our very heels. My heart beat like a wild bird's, and as to holding myself to a walk—I could hardly keep from dragging Innes after me, especially as the lights came nearer.

"A child is crying," Innes said suddenly.

"We're near the first house, close enough to throw a wicked turnip over it."

"If we had any wicked turnips, we would not be throwing them away. But we need a place to sleep. A haycock, or a church would be better. Or a stable, if it is apart from the house. And no horses."

"I see just the place."

We spent the night in a mill— "You seem to like mills," said Innes—having dragged sacks around us for bedding. The nurse's herbs had closed Innes's wound well, so just a speckling of blood dotted the bandage. I settled him down, one sack under his arm to hold it still, and before I had dragged my own sacks into place, he was asleep. I lay down beside him, shivering into his warmth.

And I fell instantly into a dream.

It was a dream that I remembered as soon as it came. I was being held tightly, tightly, by someone who loved me more than all the world, in a room that was thick with quiet and shadow, so thick I could hardly breathe. Perhaps there was something over my mouth or perhaps there was not enough air. Then the shadows fled out of the room, leaving a nothingness that filled with sudden light. It brought with it a screaming, or a roaring. Both. And then suddenly who-ever held me was gone, and the light grew brighter and brighter, and I realized with terror that I was absolutely alone in the world. That there was no one but me and this appalling light. Then a rush, and I was torn away.

I woke up, panting, filled with dread even as the dream receded. It had been as familiar as a memory.

The light that filtered through the wheat dust showed high morning. From outside came the sounds of a village at work: the creaks and groans of wooden wheels across grav-el, the lowing of oxen, the brilliant notes of a blacksmith's hammer, the voices of folks passing beneath, voices that sounded urgent, even fearful.

I woke Innes, and we brushed the mill dust from ourselves—as much as we could. "I missed the dawn," yawned
Innes.

"You'll wake to others."

He smiled ruefully. "There was a time when I was surer
of that than I am now."

"You'll be sure of it again." I laughed. "Even I'd be surer
of it if we had another jug of hot cider." Then I turned to
the ladder and saw the startled face of a miller staring at us.
A long moment passed.

"We haven't disturbed but a few sacks of meal, and those
set right easily," I said.

He continued to stare at us.

"We needed a place for the night. A place to sleep."

Still the miller did not move, standing on the ladder, a
sack of flour slung over his shoulder. He stood as though
sculpted, and I began to wonder if he might be deaf.

"We're on our way to the abbey at Saint Eynsham," I
said, trying to fill the silence with words.

Then I knew that the miller was not deaf.

"Saint Eynsham? The abbey at Saint Eynsham, you
say?"

"Yes, Saint Eynsham Abbey."

"And is this one blind, then? Have him step into the
light. It is you. To be sure, it is. There won't be a soul in this
village that doesn't look at you and know the truth of it.
You're the ones Lord Beryn's Guard warned about."

"Lord Beryn's Guard?" asked Innes.

"Wasn't it noontime just yesterday that Lord Beryn's
Guard came questioning for two boys on their way to Saint
Eynsham Abbey? And didn't they rush through our village
like locusts, searching them out? And didn't they promise to

come back with torches if they heard of us hiding the two of you?"

"No word needs to reach them."

"You'll not be understanding, boy," said the miller, shaking his head. "Not understanding at all. The one who finds you is promised riches beyond his imagining."

"So have you found us, then, for riches beyond your imagining?" asked Innes quietly.

"Me?" said the miller, surprised. He looked at us for a long time, his face considering. "Me?" he said again. Then he seemed to come to a decision. He clambered heavily up the ladder and unloaded the sack off his shoulder. "How would I be knowing if two boys were hidden in my flour mill, hidden till nightfall so they wouldn't be spied by anyone else who would give them away? Now, how would I be knowing that indeed?" And the miller waddled down the ladder and hurried out.

I settled back down on the meal. "I wonder if he'll bring us food."

"We should not stay here."

"Didn't you hear him? He's telling us to wait here so that no one will find us out."

"He's telling us to wait here, that's true enough."

"Innes, we have to trust him. We still need to find the way to the abbey. And if Lord Beryn's Guard is looking for us, and the Grip, we'll be caught if we blunder about in daylight."

"We'll be caught if he brings someone back with him."

I ignored that. "We've four days left after today. If Saint Eynsham is close, that will be time and enough to reach the abbey, hear the riddle's answer, and return to Wolverham."

"Time enough if Eynsham is close, if the queen will see

us, if she will have the riddle's answer, and if the king will let us return with it."

"Let us return with it? Of course he will." I paused, exasperated. "Innes, is this a game?"

"Never in life, Tousle. Never a game."

"But it is a game," came a new voice from the ladder. I jerked up.

First came the miller, red-faced, not looking at us. Then, huge and dark, the King's Grip. I stood and looked at the miller, but he would not meet my eyes. He held his hands out, then clasped them. "Riches beyond imagining," he said weakly, and climbed back onto the ladder.

"Remember, miller," called the King's Grip after him, "you are to tell no one about these boys. No one. Not even Lord Beryn's Guard."

"And my reward?"

"Is greater than your imagining."

The miller nodded and descended.

"Another mill," smiled the King's Grip. "Well, the merry chase comes to an end, as all merry chases must. And a merry chase it has been, boys. A merry chase indeed. And all done so quietly that none will know that it was done at all. Even the mill will seem to have simply caught fire and fallen into itself."

"You burned the mill," I accused.

"The mill, and the little cottage in the woods. Not a beam worth saving by now. Unlike the king, I always keep my promises."

"So the king never meant to give us the seven days," said Innes.

The Grip laughed roughly, his arms crossed in front of him. "It's not just your eyes that are blind," he mocked.

"And you be still," he said to me. "It hardly suits my purposes to kill, though those purposes may change."

"The king did promise us seven days," I insisted. "Seven days."

But the King's Grip laughed again. "He did indeed."

"I've heard the riddle too," said Innes. "Even if you take Tousle, I'll still solve it and be back in the courtyard."

At this a deep and guttural guffawing from the Grip filled the mill. "I've no doubt that you will, boy, blind as you are. No doubt at all."

"Then you will have failed."

"I haven't followed you across a frozen countryside for a riddle."

"You're not from the king at all," said Innes suddenly.

"Ah, not so blind after all," agreed the Grip. He leaned back against the wall.

"From Lord Beryn, then," said Innes.

"It is fitting that Lord Beryn's living memorial should be more perceptive than the king himself—though there is no great challenge there." The King's Grip was sneering. "He sent me to guard you on your way."

"A lie," I said.

"No, no indeed. There's the great joke of it. He *wants* you to solve the riddle. But when he sent me after you, he had not considered that Lord Beryn might send me to find you for a very different reason." He fingered his sword.

"The king sent you to guard us?" Innes said wonderingly.

"To guard us from what?" I asked.

"You still do not see. Not even now. To the Great Lords you are a past revealed, a maze unraveled, a darkness illuminated. You are a threat."

"Now *you* speak in riddles," said Innes.

"If riddles are the stuff of the king, then they may be the stuff of the King's Grip. This much is certain: The reward that each offers is no riddle." The smile never left the Grip's face. He stood with arms crossed, as powerful as a mountain torrent, playing with us like the silvery fish it washes away.

"Would Lord Beryn have us killed?" asked Innes.

"He would."

"And you would kill for money, for a reward beyond your imagining." The scorn in Innes's voice was as heavy as a millstone.

"Death comes with war, disease, old age, and money, boy. Only the money brings pleasure—sometimes the war."

"So," I said, "either protect us in the king's name, and take his reward, or kill us in Lord Beryn's name and take his reward. Who offered more?"

"A bold question, young Tousle. Boldly stated, and worthy of you. Would that I could do both and collect two rewards."

"No," said Innes suddenly. "No. If he had come from the king to protect us, he would not have played this game. If he came from Lord Beryn to kill us . . ."

"I would have done it. Not blind at all."

"Tousle," said Innes urgently, "the people in this village, they fear Lord Beryn's Guard, not this man. And he wants the Guard not to know about us. Don't you see? Whatever he is doing, neither the king nor Lord Beryn knows about it."

The smile dropped from the King's Grip. "Be still, boy, or the hand that blinded you will be the hand that silences you forever. Yes, riddle upon riddle, this day of the world. The game thickens and thickens."

He drew his sword and grabbed my arm. "I have a better tale to tell, a tale hidden from all but a few. The hidden tale of a tiny little man with a long tipped beard who came into the castle unnoticed by the king, by the Great Lords, by all of Lord Beryn's Guard. A tale about rooms of straw, a spinning wheel, skeins of gold thread, and the hands not of a queen but of a little man. Bales and bales of gold so fine, so perfect that no one had ever seen its like."

And then I knew. "It's Da you want. Not us. Da."

"For years I've looked for him, boy, for years. Not a day has gone by when my spies did not haunt the palace, Wolverham, the countryside. For thirteen years they have stood in shadows, along dark paths, by the city gates, watching, waiting. Thirteen years is a long time to wait. Then, at the king's procession, the news came. He was back, and with a boy. But he was gone before I could reach him, vanished before I could even leave the castle." He grabbed my arm even harder. "But by chance or design, the boy was left behind."

"By design. To answer a riddle."

"Damn the king and damn his riddling. Do you think I run his errands like a hound? Or fly from the hand of Lord Beryn like a falcon to make his kill?"

"No," said Innes quietly. "All you want is the gold."

"Bales and bales of it," answered the Grip.

With a leer on his face and gold in his eyes, the King's Grip loomed over me. And yet he seemed much smaller. Before, he had carried the weight of the king's will. Now he was only a greedy traitor who wanted to know the secret of spinning straw into gold.

But it hardly mattered. We had failed to answer the riddle. Whether the King's Grip took me, or whether we were both caught by Lord Beryn's Guard, the ending would be the same. Four days from now, the riddle unanswered, the rebels would be hanged at the castle. And all the riddles in the world would no longer matter to them. That world suddenly seemed too large for me. A terrible longing seized me for Da and for my old quiet home that had disappeared in such a very short time. I shivered with the loss.

"So now," the Grip said to Innes, "I leave you with more riddles than you began with. Fly away and solve them—that is, if the good people of Twickenham do not hand you over to Lord Beryn's Guard for the reward beyond imagining. See if they will take pity on someone the King's Grip has blinded." And he turned me to the ladder.

That was when Innes said the one thing that neither the Grip nor I could ever have expected. He said it quietly and evenly, standing with his hands held open. He said it like a benediction: "I've forgiven the blinding." And as he stood, his arm held a bit crooked, his body covered with the dust and sweat of the last days, I thought with a start how much he looked like the golden king.

The Grip stopped, his hand still tight. He did not turn around. When I looked at his face, I saw it curling into a snarl. But I also saw what it curled from: amazement.

"As if I had need of your forgiveness," the King's Grip whispered.

"Perhaps not. The need to forgive was my own," answered Innes.

Now the King's Grip did turn to him, and the snarl had vanished. "Do you know who you are, boy?"

"Innes, the blind fool."

A long time passed, the mill dust twirling in the sunlight, the sounds of the village going on. The Grip watched Innes, and for a wild moment I thought he might weep. He opened his mouth as if to speak but paused again. He almost seemed to want to touch him. Then, finally, he spoke, slowly and even sadly. "The day might have been when I would have bowed my knee to such a blind fool. And bowed it gladly. But that day is gone forever." He gathered himself and pushed me toward the ladder. "As for me"—he waved his free hand in the air— "forgive someone who wants forgiveness."

Innes said nothing more.

Instead, he lowered his shoulder and sprinted headlong into our backs, battering me down and the Grip through the ladder's opening. With a shout the Grip flailed at the frame, then half slid, half rolled down, crashing from step to step until he struck with a squashy thud against the stone floor.

Innes, breathing heavily, whispered, "Tousle?"

I looked down the ladder and tried to focus my eyes. "No need to whisper. He won't be hearing us." I looked down again. He was not moving. "Now he has something to forgive."

"Is he dead?"

"Just a little bit more than me. Couldn't you have told me what you were about to do?"

"I didn't suppose he would give us a private moment to plan our escape."

I stood up, running my fingers along my ribs to see if they were hurting only because they were bruised. "He shouldn't be after us again."

"There are still Lord Beryn's Guard," Innes pointed out.

"Innes," I said, "you needn't always leap to point out the difficulties."

"Then here's one happy leap: You were right. The king wants us to solve the riddle."

The ribs seemed bruised only.

"But now there's the other riddle," Innes continued. "The king must know that Lord Beryn wants us to fail, or he wouldn't have sent the Grip to guard us. So why should Lord Beryn oppose the king?"

My head was starting to throb, and when I rubbed the back of it, I was hardly surprised to find the bump, could almost feel it swelling under my fingers. "Innes, we'll answer the king's riddle first. The Grip must have left his horse outside."

Innes paused a long moment. "And if he has?"

"Then we'll ride it to Saint Eynsham Abbey, Innes." I sighed.

"Are you remembering that horses are afraid of me?"

"Yes, terrified."

We clambered down the ladder and stepped over the Grip. Still no movement from him. I peered outside the mill: The Grip's black horse waited, tied to a post. As soon as he saw me, he began pawing at the ground.

"I'll stay quiet," said Innes.

I held my palms out and, one slow step at a time, moved toward the horse, clucking my tongue.

"Horse," I whispered, "you may be our way to Saint Eynsham Abbey. You'll save our feet. And who knows how many you'll save in Wolverham."

The horse looked up again. He seemed to understand.

"If you get us there, we'll sing about you in songs, call our best colts by your name, and tell your story on a cold winter's night."

Slowly, slowly I unwound his reins from about the post.

"'The Glory of the Black Steed,' we'll call it. It will be a story told for a hundred generations."

Half cooing, half whistling to the horse, slowly, slowly I started to gather the reins in one hand.

And slowly, slowly the horse rolled his head, pulled the reins from my hands, and ambled away.

I broke into a run. He broke into a slow canter. I went into a full sprint, and he went into a light, prancing gallop and waggled his fat hind end just as he disappeared into the woods. I flung a rock, but it missed his last waggle.

Innes was waiting patiently when I came back, winded. "I don't think he likes that noise you make with your tongue," he said.

"We need to cross the village and find the road on the far side. I can see it easily enough from here. It borders five, six, seven fields and then finds the woods."

"Is there anyone at work in the fields?"

"No one."

"And between us and the fields?"

"I see a long barn, the church, another barn beside a round barn, the manor house, the commons, then a row of houses, maybe ten or twelve."

"Perhaps if we waited till dark."

"And I see Lord Beryn's Guard just coming out of the woods."

"Anything else?"

"Nothing but the miller, who is hurrying off to meet them."

"Perhaps he is off to sell them some bread."

"Not bread," I said. "You know, Innes, I've spent whole days in my life when nothing ever happened to me."

"See what you've missed by not being blind. Maybe we should try to hide in the church."

Crouching, we ran toward the village. I was surprised at how suddenly the day seemed very, very bright, and how the light sharpened everything. Every branch was glinting with last night's hard frost. The stubble that stood in the fields stuck brusquely up and caught the light full. The air was perfectly blue, so blue that it startled the black trees to attention.

And even as my breath came shorter and shorter, I realized that deep inside, in a place touched only rarely, I was gladdened by the world, and gladdened by Innes. Even with Lord Beryn's Guard coming into the village behind us.

We crossed to the barn and creaked the door open. Rows of cows raised their heavy heads to us, then returned to their slow chewing. Fresh hay lay on the flooring, and a pitchfork was propped against one stall.

"Someone will be coming back soon, so let's be quick. Don't step there, Innes."

Through another door at the far end of the barn, then across to the church, a pause under the stone archway, then a push through the door, and we were in. The heavily spiced darkness of the place came around us. It might as well have been night outside, for all the light that shone here. Tiers of thick white candles lit the far end where the altar stood, their waxy smell spreading through the church, but their light huddled under the darkness sinking from the roof. It was all as quiet and as still as could be.

"I think we're alone," I whispered.

"No," said Innes, shaking his head.

"Who is ever alone in a church, children?" said another voice, and I saw someone rising from his knees in the center aisle, his robe blending so perfectly with the darkness that I had not seen him. He stood as quiet and as still as the church around him. His robe was belted tight—he looked as though he fasted regularly—and the low light of the candles set a halo around his head. In that holy place he seemed more spirit than body.

"Those who flee are safe here," he said slowly.

"Even two hiding from Lord Beryn's Guard?" asked Innes.

"Most especially two hiding from Lord Beryn's Guard. But most houses in Twickenham would have been a safe place. Not all—some are tempted beyond their mortal will—but most. Have the Guard returned?"

"They have," I said.

He asked nothing more, but beckoning, he led us deeper into the church, behind the altar and into the apse, where he set us crouching behind an altar screen. He motioned with his hands that we were to stay, and we waited, breathing heavily, but somehow never doubting that he had the mortal will to resist the temptation of a reward beyond imagining. When he came back, he brought bread and cheese, and milk still warm from the udder. "It pleases me to think that ours might be the richest, creamiest milk in Twickenham, though I am often warned against boasting," the sexton admitted.

"Do you know the way to the abbey at Saint Eynsham?" asked Innes.

"I do. You are only a few hours away from it. I have traveled to Saint Eynsham Abbey myself."

"To the queen?" I said. "Do you know her?"

He spread his hands wide. "I was serving the abbey when she first arrived, but I am only a sexton. The small offices I have done her she would hardly remember. And she was none too eager to meet anyone then. She had just been banished to the abbey, you see, and that without her child."

"She was banished to the abbey," repeated Innes slowly.

"By the king himself. I am told he does not forgive easily.

Finish the cheese now. You'll not be disturbed here. Even Lord Beryn's Guard would not desecrate the altar—though there's one who would, if he knew you were here. At nightfall you'll come to my house. You'll eat again and grow warm."

But it wasn't eating and warming that first met us that night. The sexton came back for us late, carrying two cloaks the color of gray night. We scurried through the dark and moonless night, so dark that even the stars seemed to shine no light. We followed his sure steps to a whitewashed cottage, the door opened to a gleam of yellow light, and he shoved us in. "Wife," he whispered. There was a moment of utter quiet, then a high squeal of such pitch that piglets could hardly have matched it. "By Saint Julian himself, it can hardly be true. Can it be true? It cannot, yet it is," and by the time she had finished, we were encased in the nurse's arms and drawn into her, and she was murmuring at us and crying and laughing, as if we had been her long-lost babes, returned to her arms at last and ready to remember her own dear lullaby.

Then there was more food—mutton and cold ham and eggs whipped to a froth—and all the while she was heating buckets of water for us, and we ate to the hot splashing of it into a copper tub. "A sight," she said, drying her hands on her apron. "You're as black as if you'd rolled with hogs. And there's other things I could say about you that would hardly be proper to say to folks so lately met." She reached above her, pulled a handful of purple herbs dangling from the beam, and threw them into the water. "You first," she said to me. "And you'll be next. Give me those smelly things you've got on. No, I'll have none of that. I've raised more than my share, and there's nothing new under the sun for me to see. So be quick about it and in you go."

I had forgotten how delicious it was to be so warm. But even more, I was surprised at how pleasing it was to have someone fuss over me. She lathered me up, wiped me down with a coarse towel, and clothed me in carefully patched clothes, all the while crooning her lovely lullaby.

And afterward there was hot cider, the tale of the Grip at the two mills, the tale of her own escape in the cart— "Saint Leoba herself must have sent her blessed bees"—and then wonder at the king and his riddling. "And the king sent the Grip to guard you?" exclaimed the nurse. "Another riddle only the queen herself might answer," she said.

But as to Lord Beryn, she knew well enough why he might set his Guard in search. "By Saint Sebastian, he is a man who hates for no reason other than to hate. Why, he hated even the queen, that gentle soul, only because she was a miller's daughter. 'I'll not be bowing my knee to a peasant,' he said aloud, and even in her presence if the king had no ear nearby. He would have killed her and the child both, if the baby hadn't disappeared first. Then he turned the king against her, and that's why she sits alone in Saint Eynsham Abbey, the dear, with never a word of those she loved."

"Can a man hate so much that he would kill a baby?" I asked.

"Yes," murmured Innes, "and worse."

The sexton rose and stood behind Innes, his hands on his shoulders. "Who knows how the hate of Lord Beryn fits into the design of all things in this world, and whether even that hatred—yes, wife, even that hatred—will take its right place. But for now, sleep."

The nurse led us to their loft and laid us down between heavy rugs, pulling them over and around us so that their fur lay thick and warm against our chests, and the sweet, heavy smell of the leather came up against our faces. She tucked the heavy comfort of it tight around us. The sexton sat by the door—he would stay there till morning—and I watched the nurse stand over him and touch her hand against his cheek.

I lay back, caught between waking and sleep, then fell gently into dreamlessness.

chapter seven

When I woke up, it was full dark. The wind outside whined as it searched for chinks in the walls, then whistled shrilly when it found one and stuck its nose through. It was a cold whistling, and I was not ready to leave the huddle of the rugs when the sexton's hand shook my shoulder.

"I'll take you to the abbey now. It's best to go soon, while it is still dark and we can see the watch fires of Lord Beryn's Guard."

I nodded, still half asleep.

"And one thing more. The Grip is not in the mill."

I was no longer half asleep. I shook Innes awake.

"His body has been moved?" But the sexton only shrugged his shoulders.

The nurse had three packs ready for us and our dark cloaks on her arms.

"There's more than one time we've taken a secret walk at night when Lord Beryn's Guard have been about," the sexton explained with a sly wink, "and we've enjoyed the venison for it all the next winter."

The nurse draped the cloaks around us and crushed each of us in turn—even the sexton.

"Be safe, be safe. And when you reach the queen, may you find her well, poor dear." She clasped us closely once more, then doused the lamps and shushed us out the door. The touch of her hand on my back stayed with me through the night.

And a dark night it was. As dark as we would have wished, and darker. Innes held on to my cloak and I followed the sexton, though it was not easy. His thin self scurried like a rabbit, the stars alone giving him enough light. We did not speak, nor did we ever slow our pace. We moved like the shadow of an owl, and as quietly, while the wind crackled together the icy branches over our heads.

Long before any light even hinted at the dawn—the beginning of our fourth day—the sexton stopped us. "A short rest," he whispered. "We'll be there soon enough, and it's then we'll see the Guard's fires."

I nodded and sat down, my back against the rough bark of a tree. Almost immediately the heat from the walking left me and the ground frost began to work its way up my back. I held my cloak close, while Innes paced back and forth, beating his arms against his sides.

"Heaven only knows how you'll find the queen," the sexton whispered. "It's been eleven years and more since I last saw her, and then she seemed like one who had fallen into herself, what with her sadness. What more years of brooding might do to her . . ." He shook his head at the thought. "She came to Twickenham once, you know, soon after she was crowned and on her way to visit the abbey nuns. Our maids danced for her, and they put flowers in her hair and she danced with them, round and round about. It seemed that hers would be the sweetest reign. Then a year later she came again, alone and at dark. On a night just as cold as this, I saw her ride into Saint Eynsham Abbey with my own eyes."

"She was alone," said Innes. It was not a question.

"She was with my own dear wife, her nurse, sent off with her, never to return to the castle. But at the king's command, the king's loving command, she was turned away at the abbey doors, and the queen walked in alone and unattended, like a peasant in search of a night's shelter. At the gate I found her nurse weeping and weeping, and there was no way to comfort her, the child being gone and the queen walled away. And so I brought her here"

"How is it the queen lost her baby?" I asked.

A long moment of silence. "You haven't heard the story?" Innes asked. "Tousle, it's one I've heard over and over again, and me just an orphan shuttled from horse stall to horse stall. How the queen bore the king's heir, and how he disappeared after a year, probably murdered. How the king banished his queen to Saint Eynsham Abbey, there to live the rest of her life unless called upon."

"I never heard the story," I said, standing and rubbing the chill out of my legs. "My da never told it."

"And now is not the time for the telling of it," said the sexton. "Not if we hope to pass Lord Beryn's Guard while the dark is still with us." And so we started again, trudging forward with numbed toes.

And the dark was still with us when the trees thinned out and showed Saint Eynsham and the abbey beyond, a low dark mass against a low dark sky. I would have not seen it if it had not been for the pale lights that flickered feebly in three of its windows.

There were no fires in the clearing between us and the

village, and no sign of Lord Beryn's Guard. Still, the sexton was cautious. "Steady now, steady now," he said from the last grouping of trees. "The Devil himself would be in it if we were to come so far and be caught at the very doors." Slowly he stepped out, stepped back in again, and then out once more. Three steps and he motioned to me to follow.

And so slowly, crouching, sometimes breaking into a run, we crossed the open ground and reached a small stream. "There," said the sexton, pointing. "Put your feet just there." But I could see almost nothing in the darkness, and though the sexton leapt from stone to stone, Innes and I were soon wet up to our knees, until we both finally simply waded across most of it. "There used to be a ford here," said the sexton.

"There isn't anymore," replied Innes. We went on, the frigid water squishing out of our shoes and our toes starting to pain as though they could crack off.

"Will we be able to get into the abbey?" I whispered.

"Will there be a fire to welcome us?" asked Innes.

The sexton held up his hand to quiet us. "If it's heard that you two have reached the abbey, it's not the getting in that you'll need to be worried about. Mind you move quiet as the tomb here, or we'll have every dog and rooster and pig in Saint Eynsham barking and cackling and squealing."

We moved past a row of houses—all dark, all sleeping—and to the commons. It was too cold for any cows to be tethered there—winter still holding on as it was—so we ran across it, startling only a few of the larks that had begun to gather. Past another row of houses, and then we stood at the top of a vale that sloped down between two rounded hills. And in the very center of that vale stood Saint Eynsham Abbey.

"Now, the way you'll want to be going . . ." began the sexton.

"A moment," whispered Innes urgently. The sky that had grown pinker and pinker as we crossed Saint Eynsham showed brighter, brighter, and then yielded to the white sun that rolled over the world's edge. And in the utter quiet, Innes stood with his face to it, rapt, still.

"Whatever is he doing?" asked the sexton.

"God's gift," I said.

The sexton nodded his head and waited patiently. "It's yours to hear the dawn, then," he said when Innes turned back to us.

"It is," said Innes surprised. "How would you know that?"

The sexton leaned forward and mussed his hair. "You're hardly the only one God is giving gifts to. How do you think that I'm able to find my way through the woods on the darkest night?" Then, as the larks began to sing, he pointed down the vale to the abbey.

I felt alone. In all this wide world, was everyone so sure of his gift but me?

The path out of Saint Eynsham meandered to a stone-arched door, the only opening in a wall three times as high as a man. The wall rounded the abbey in gracious curves, heading up a rise and curling at the top of the gorge, then coming back through lowland and around again up a bare hill, finally closing its loop at the end of a sturdy limestone church, the cross on its roof like a key locking it all together.

"That over there is the abbey church," said the sexton pointing, "and a finer one you'll never see this side of Wolverham. Follow along the wall there, and you see Saint Joseph's Chapel, Saint Mary's Chapel, and there, the smallest, Saint Anne's. If I were to make a guess, it would be to Saint Anne's that the queen goes to say her prayers.

"Now, follow the line of these cherry trees across the court. The cherry trees, Tousle, not the pear. Right. At the far end is the abbess's house. The grand one. Just to the south of it—no, to the south, boy—there's the abbey hall. It's where the Holy Sisters will be when they are not at prayers. It's where they do most of their living."

"And that is where the queen will be?" asked Innes.

"It may be that she would be there. But, Tousle, if you look back to Saint Anne's Chapel, you see where there has been new building? It's my guess that those are the queen's rooms."

I stared down at the abbey grounds. The first sunbeams had already scampered past the ordered fruit trees—pear and cherry—and clambered all around the chapel steeples, and finally lay against Saint Anne's, where they were beginning to dry the dew from the dark slate.

"Then I'll be leaving you here, Tousle, and you, Innes. You'll find an attendant at the door, and she'll welcome you, though I'm of a mind that she'll not take you to the queen. You'll need to find that way yourselves. But if you do come to meet the queen, if you do, give her a blessing from me, and tell her that I well remember the sad night that brought her here."

A pause.

"And I'll be remembering you both as well."

"And we you," whispered Innes.

"We'll be back," I said. "When the riddle is solved and we've taken it to Wolverham, we'll be back."

The sexton raised his hand in blessing and farewell, and left us looking down on Saint Eynsham Abbey.

The sexton was wrong about the attendant. Though all the limestone apostles smiled down from their cozy niches, the iron hinges on the oak door did not creak open with a welcome. Instead, a tiny window jutted open at our third knocking and a face thrust out, a face as solid as the rounded stones that arched the door. It might almost have been made of rock itself.

"As if we haven't had enough visitors these last three days," she shouted. "As if all I have to do is to unbolt and unbar the door to any wretch who comes along and chooses to knock."

"Isn't it to the wretched that the abbey doors should open?" asked Innes.

She glared at him. "Boy, there's a warm hearth and a hot rum I've left for your knocking. I'm thinking it a trial and a tribulation to have done so."

"Mother," I called quickly, when I saw her hands move up to close the portal, "we've traveled through the night and are only looking for a bit of warm fire."

"A bit of warm fire," she repeated. "And some bread to go with it?"

"Well, yes."

She nodded. "Some stew perhaps, steaming for all it's worth? Maybe some of my hot rum?"

"Yes, again."

"Beggars," she spat, and reached to pull the window shut.

"Wait!" I shouted. "We're not beggars. We've come all the way from Wolverham to see the queen."

Innes groaned.

"Ah, the queen," repeated the attendant. "And perhaps you'd wish to see the mother abbess after you've made your royal visit."

"No," I said.

"And then you'll be off to bless the Holy Father in Rome?" she asked sweetly.

"We must see the queen," said Innes urgently. "We've come from the king himself."

"So a troop of Lord Beryn's Guard claimed only yesterday morning, but she would not see them—and the door stayed closed. So another one, rougher than you've ever seen the likes of, said yesterday evening, but she would not see him—and the door stayed closed. The queen has seen precious few these last eleven years. She'll not be changing her ways simply to see beggars looking for a fire."

"She might," said Innes, drawing himself up tall. "Tell her that her son is here to see her."

If the clouds had suddenly turned leaden and dropped with a clang onto the abbey, I could hardly have been more surprised.

"She will be displeased should you keep me from her," added Innes.

The attendant slanted her head and peered down at us warily. "And where's the proof of this?"

"The heart has no need of proof. Tell her."

For a long moment she stared at Innes. "Is there a likeness?" she muttered to herself, and leaning back, she closed the window and was gone.

"The queen's son?" I asked.

Innes shrugged. "If she wouldn't open the door to Lord Beryn's Guard, what chance did we have as beggars?"

"The queen will know that you're not her son."

"But we'll be in the abbey, face to face. At least we can ask her the riddle."

"The queen will dismiss us as soon as she sees us."

"Tousle, you needn't always leap to point out the difficulties. This might be the only way to find the answer to the riddle."

"Well, then," I said, "you should look the part." I took off the square-linked chain that Da had put around my neck and secured it around Innes's. He put his hand up to feel its cold metal.

"Does this make me look the part of a prince?"

"Not much."

Innes grinned as the door to the abbey swung slowly open and the attendant beckoned us in. She led us across the courtyard, turning now and again to eye us suspiciously, as if we were there to make off with the abbey's treasures. And she must have told others of Innes's claim, for though Holy Sisters glided past with downcast faces, some murmuring prayers, they all turned their faces up at the last moment to catch a glimpse of us.

Across the courtyard a stand of cherry trees had already started to bud. It seemed impossible for this time of year, yet there they were, their branches supple and starting to swell, as if in that protected corner of the world, the sun shone warmer and the cold winds swirled away. I imagined the scent of them blossomed out, and the shower of soft petals they would yield soon. I kept the thought close when we came to Saint Anne's Chapel and the attendant opened the door for us, then stood aside to let us in—still suspicious.

I took Innes's elbow and led him into the sweet half darkness of the place. Slants of sunshine colored through the windows, but the sun was still too low for the beams to angle down to the floor. They floated high, a rainbow of light, like a canopy over us. Beneath them the air was heavy with the waxy scent of glowing candles and the spiced tinge of incense.

At the far end of the chapel a wooden statue of Saint

Anne paused above rows and rows of candles, her arms outstretched and open as if to welcome the Holy Child. And beneath her, just rising and smoothing her gown, was the queen.

She stood, a dark pillar in front of the candles, her hands clasped in front of her, not moving. I could not see her face in the dimness of the place, but in her solemn stillness she bespoke royalty, and I knelt, pulling Innes down with me.

"Come closer," she said, her voice low, almost husky.

We did, passing through slices of colored light. Kneeling before her, I could see that she was not young. She had been beautiful, but no longer. She looked like someone who had cried until she found that crying brought no relief, and she had stopped not because the sadness was past, but because the sadness had no remedy.

"Closer still," she said, and we rose and stood within arm's reach.

"The boy from Wolverham who would defy a king to ask mercy for others," she said quietly.

"Yes, Majesty."

Then she turned to Innes. She lifted her hand and laid it across his face, running her fingertips along the scar that creased through his eyes. She brushed his dark hair back lightly from his forehead.   *

"So it is you who claim to be my son." She shook her head. "How I wish it were true. For eleven years I have longed for him, stroked his hair just so in my mind's eye time and time and time again, and sung to him the songs that his nurse taught me to sing while I carried him in my womb." She looked back at Saint Anne behind her. "How many times have I implored the saint to bring my son to me, and how many times has she not brought him."

"Majesty," began Innes.

She turned back to us. "And now you come. But how can I tell if you are from the saint or just another temptation? How can I let myself hope, when if this hope too comes to nothing, it will carry away with it all faith entirely?"

Innes's face wrinkled to a tightness.

"Majesty," I said, "we have come from Wolverham, from the king, with a riddle to solve."

"He was ever fond of riddles," she answered, her fingers on Innes's face again. "There is a likeness indeed here. And your hair is the right color."

"We are to answer the riddle if we are to save the lives of those in rebellion against the Great Lords."

The queen continued to stroke Innes's face, stroking and stroking. "Where is it you come from?" she asked.

"Wolverham, Majesty," I answered.

She nodded her head, but if she had heard, the answer meant little to her.

"With a riddle," I added.

But the queen gave no answer. Her fingers stopped, and she stared at Innes, as if trying to pierce her own blindness, as if she would dare to let herself for a moment believe, while knowing that believing was to give her hope its very last chance. She turned back over her shoulder to Saint Anne, now lit brightly by the growing sunlight, then turned again to Innes.

"How is it that I'm to know?" she asked slowly. "How is it that I'm ever to know?"

At this, Innes dropped to his knees. "Majesty, forgive us. We never meant to bring hurt, but we would say anything to see you. Anything to answer the riddle."

The queen dropped her hand from Innes's face, and I

waited for the disdainful dismissal she would give us. She had not even heard the riddle, let alone given us an answer, and I imagined the long trek back to Wolverham—if we would make it back to Wolverham—with an unsure answer from the miller.

But the queen had not dropped her hand because of Innes's plea. Trembling, she reached out and took the square-linked chain with the tips of her fingers. She looked at it with open, puzzled eyes. "How can this be? This is not yours."

"No, Majesty."

"How did you come by it?" she insisted.

"It is mine," I said.

She turned to me, and she was trembling. "Yours?"

"It was given to me, by my da."

"Not your mother?"

"I never knew her."

The queen let the necklace drop against Innes's chest. She took me by the shoulders and pressed her hands against my cheekbones. Her eyes were still large, and now even wild. She looked back and forth from us to Saint Anne, her hand trembling so that it shook like an autumn leaf about to lose its hold. "How can this be?" she said again. "One has the likeness but the other the necklace. I do not know. I do not know. And by all that is holy, I am afraid to hope without proof."

"The heart has no need of proof," said Innes quietly.

The queen looked once at Innes, then back to me. "The necklace," she said with a gasp, "is my own." Slowly she put an arm around my shaking self. And slowly she reached her other arm out and drew Innes to her. Then she drew us both tighter, tighter, tighter, as if she would take us into her. A great sob filled the chapel, a great and terrible sob that carried with it all the longing and pain of lonely years. She held on to us both as though there were nothing else in the world worth holding on to.

Innes reached around her and laid his head against her breast. Her hand reached into his hair, and he began to sob.

And I too yielded. Whether or not I was her son, I could have done nothing but yield. I put my arms around her, as tight as her own, and under the outstretched hands of Saint Anne, we all three wept with the terrible fullness that had seized us. We wept together, letting tears overwhelm us and carry us away like a tide, drowning in our hope and glad of the drowning, afraid to separate because we might find ourselves alive again in a world without a mother, without a son.

Lord forgive me, Lord forgive me, there was a part of me, and not a tiny part, that wished that Innes were not here, that the queen and I were alone.

But there was another part, and a bigger one, that grew more and more solid as we stood in that holy place. If I had wished, for a moment, that I was the one who had found his mother, I could also wish that it might be Innes who had found her. Even though it would shatter the bright prism of my own joy, I could still wish it.

Perhaps our greatest groans are for those things that we wish to give away.

So we stood in one another's arms as the brilliant light slanted closer and closer around us, until finally it covered us all in ruby and amethyst hues, before moving once again down to the shadows.

chapter eight

I do not know how long we might have stood there, bathed in that bright slanting light, holding on so tightly that our fingers ached with the strain of it. But the world never does stop, not for joy, not for sorrow. And finally the queen stepped back and laid her hands against our faces. "Have you been happy?" she asked. "Have you both been happy?"

I nodded. But Innes did not. Gently she laid her forehead against his and seemed to breathe into him. "I have been so alone," he said.

She nodded. She understood.

"And you?" Innes asked. "Have you been happy?"

"Not for a long time. I am not sure that I even remember what it is to be happy." She paused, considering. "I comforted myself with the thought that if my son was no longer in my hands, so too was he out of the hands of the Great Lords. But it was only cold comfort."

"Majesty," said Innes, "I cannot say that I am your son."

"Nor can I," I said.

She smiled at us both. "Nor can I say that I am your mother." She dropped her warm palms from our cheeks and grasped our hands. "But here I am, and here you are. And after all, nothing is ever quite by chance."

The words startled me to silence. I had heard them before.

"Majesty," asked Innes, "do you know what happened to your son?"

A long moment passed.

"I let him be taken," she said finally. "I let him be taken. Taken by a tiny little man with a strange and curious gait, and eyes that popped out like a frog's, and fingers as long as spindles. He riddled me for his name, and when I could not answer his riddle, he carried my son away in a basket." She spoke very quietly now. "He was asleep and did not even see me as the little man left." Her hands went to her face, and in the silence she heaved a sob so long, so grieved, that it seemed her soul was flying from her.

A hand reached out and seized my heart. It began to squeeze.

And all the while Saint Anne looked down upon us, and the holy candles flickered.

"Did you hate him?" I asked in a whisper.

She nodded. "I came to this chapel to practice hate. And there was so much to practice upon. A fool of a father who made an idle boast. A cowardly husband who feared more than he loved. A tiny man who clutched my baby to himself." She looked up at the saint. "But I found something else here too, something I did not expect." She leaned down and whispered. "What if it was love that took away my child and banished me from the castle?"

"It was not love," I said.

She smiled. "For eleven years I have pondered these things and told no one, except her." She nodded back to Saint Anne. "What if it was love? What if my child was taken to protect him from the Great Lords? What if a king, who feared so much that he pushed even happiness away, banished his queen so she too would be safe from them? What if it was love?"

"Then you could forgive," said Innes.

She looked at both of us, and again her eyes filled. "Then I could forgive. And perhaps the day might come when there would be even more."

Bells rang, and the queen looked around the chapel. "But we have forgotten the day." She passed her hands over her face once, then again, and together we walked out into a gentle swaddling of sunlight. We stood for a moment by the side of Saint Anne's Chapel, in a sunny spot whose grass had warmed to a green.

Innes's arms were tight around his chest, as if he were holding himself together, and when I looked at the queen in that first light, I knew that I was not the queen's own son. God in heaven, I was not.

And oddly enough, the hand that had gripped my heart loosened.

"What spins out now took its place on the wheel long ago," Da had said. In this guarded spot, near the swelling fruit trees—cherry or peach or whatever they were—I wondered what pattern was being woven for me—what pattern *I* might weave for me.

"Majesty," Innes said at last, "shall I return your necklace?"

"No," she said gently. "It looks all the better on you—though it is no longer mine to give or to take."

"It is yours," I said to Innes. "The little man told me

that I would know when to give it away. So now it is yours."

"The little man?" the queen asked.

"The little man with the strange and curious gait, the eyes that pop out like a frog's, and the fingers as long as spindles."

"The little man told you to give it away?"

"Yes, Majesty."

"But how could you have known him?"

"Majesty, he is my da." She stared at me. "Nothing is ever quite by chance," I repeated.

"You are sure that . . ."

"I am, Majesty."

"Such a strange thing," she murmured, "that he would say that." She looked deeply into me.

"The necklace, Majesty, belongs to Innes," I said simply.

And she nodded. She knew. She knew. She knew beyond hope. Everything in her spirit rang its truth. She turned to Innes with a joy august and giddy at the same time, a joy that sounded like the bells of the dawn. She reached out to him, then looked at me. I smiled, and then she filled his hands with her own.

The sun was now shining fully onto the abbey grounds, and from one of the chapels came the tones of chanted prayers, low and even. I wondered how many days had passed here just like this one, always the same quiet lapping of the hours, one day softly rippling into the next. There must have been a time when the abbey chapels were being built, but now they looked as if their stones had simply emerged from a clearing fog one primeval day, and as if the warming sun had drawn the moss and ivy up from the ground to soften and green the edges. Nothing seemed to have changed here for a very long time.

Except on this day.

"Majesty," said Innes, "we still have the riddle from the king."

She smiled, almost laughed, hardly able to keep from picking him up and cradling him to her. Perhaps she did not because she did not have the strong heft of the nurse. Or perhaps she did not because she knew it might hurt me. Perhaps it would have.

"And what is the riddle?" she asked.

"What fills a hand fuller than a skein of gold?" Innes recited.

And then she was no longer laughing. "Is this from the king?"

"It is."

She looked at me. "And when he gave it, was he mocking?"

"No," I said. "There was no mocking in his eyes. There was . . ."

"Yes? What was in his eyes?"

"Majesty, I think he was hoping we might solve the riddle."

"Perhaps he had hope for even more." She stepped away from us and reached up into the boughs of a cherry tree, pulling a branch down to her. Its buds were filling with the juice of early spring, and she fingered one carefully. "The riddle," she asked, "was it given in the presence of the Great Lords?"

I nodded.

"And Lord Beryn. He heard the riddle?"

"Yes, Majesty."

"Majesty," asked Innes slowly, "do you know the answer?"

She looked at him and again took his hands in hers. "Since the day the king sent me from the castle, I have been called back to Wolverham only a handful of days. And on each of those days, the Great Lords have not allowed me to speak to him alone. Never once. They listen to all his words, they watch all he does. But they cannot read his eyes. And reading eyes is something a miller's daughter learns to do if she is to know which of her customers has weighed his grain truly and which not."

"Majesty," said Innes, "did the king's eyes tell you that he was banishing you from the castle because he loved you?"

The queen's startled hand went to her heart, and she looked at Innes with puzzlement.

"Do you know the answer to the riddle?" I asked quietly.

"I do," she said slowly.

"Then tell us," insisted Innes, "and we will take it back to Wolverham."

"The answer is not for telling," she replied. "I will take it back to Wolverham with you. We will stand together, the three of us, and we will see if the king truly wishes to hear the riddle's answer. We will see if he wants his happiness more than his fear."

"He does," I said. "He would not have sent his Grip to guard us along the way if he did not."

"The King's Grip brought you here? That is not possible."

"No, Majesty," said Innes, and he told her the story of our last four days. She wept when she heard of the miller's decision to hold the King's Grip so that we might escape. And she laughed through her tears when he told of the sexton and the nurse who had hidden us. She watched us as though he were telling her her own life.

"The king never understood the hunger that gold and power make. He could not understand that there might be some who thought these of less worth than other things," she said wonderingly when he finished.

"Majesty," said Innes, "if he truly wants us to answer the riddle, then he knows." At this, the queen smiled.

"When must we be in Wolverham?"

"By dawn, three days from now."

"Then we need not hurry. The abbey will lend us the horses we need, and we are only a long day's ride from the city. Innes, are you ill?"

"No, Majesty. Not ill. It's just that . . ."

"Horses are afraid of him," I supplied.

"These are gentle horses," she said.

"So I have been told more than once. Your pardon, but it is never so."

She smiled, even laughed, and took him by the shoulders and drew him to her. She held him tightly, tightly. Then she bent down and kissed one eye, and then the other.

A loud and insistent pounding upon the oak door of the abbey grounds. When it was not answered immediately, a louder pounding, so thick and so powerful that it seemed as if the door must spring open. The Holy Sisters looked up from their low prayers, and as the attendant hustled to the door, the queen held Innes's head against her. Scolding, the attendant opened the window, then fell back before the roar that careened in. A mailed arm reached through, fumbled for the bolt, and slid it open. With a crash the door was kicked back against the inner wall.

And Lord Beryn strode into the abbey courtyard.

He stood still and large, his arms angled against his hips. He seemed like one who had come to conquer. When the mother abbess came out to him, floating across the court-yard, he waited unmoving, his legs spread on the cobble-stones. He looked down at her like a mountain upon low hills. "I will see the queen," he said. "No, Mother, there will be no denial this time. I will see her now. The men I prom-ised have arrived. They are tired after a long night's ride, and cold and hungry. It is for you to say whether they will set up their tents on the common of Saint Eynsham, or whether they will find warmer lodgings here, among you." He looked around. "It seems a well-stocked place, and their comfort is much on my mind."

Then he saw us.

The smile that creased his face was the smile the demons wear when a new soul falls to hell.

"Lord Beryn," said the queen, standing in front of us, "do not look so. One would think that you had eaten some-thing foul."

"Mistress Miller," he called, "I will not bandy words with you."

"If you are ill, seek out Sister Margaret, who will provide the emetic you need." She turned away from him and held her hand out for me.

Waving the mother abbess aside, Lord Beryn crossed the courtyard and stood under the cherry trees with us. His voice dropped. "Mistress Miller, I come for the boy."

The queen's hands gripped us both. "Indeed, you do not bandy words."

"You know the Great Lords will not allow the succession to go through a peasant mother. We will not bow our knees to a peasant king."

"My son is the king's son."

Lord Beryn laughed. "If I had had my way, there would

have been no son. The king would have had his skeins of gold to play with the livelong day, and you would have been dismissed for your troubles, with a bauble on your finger to entice some herdsman to wed you. But the king fancied himself in love."

"And who are you to say what is fancy? Who are you to say that love of gold cannot quickly become as cold and dead as yellow metal, and that someone—even a king—can turn his love elsewhere?"

Lord Beryn scoffed. "It does not matter now whether his love was fancied or real. Let it be real, if you will. If so, chance was kinder to you than you deserved."

"The king's riddle shows that it is real," said the queen.

"And it is for that riddle, Mistress Miller, that I have come. I will take the boy now."

The queen turned back to face Lord Beryn, and she stood as if a crown would be more natural on her head than the kerchief of a miller's daughter. The moment had made her larger, and almost I wondered if her head would scrape against the cherry boughs.

"No," she said simply. "No."

"Mistress Miller, I have told you that I would not bandy words, and I will not. I will not commit sacrilege in this sanctuary, but neither will I allow you ever to leave it, nor these two. It is your peril I speak of. Yield the child."

And at the words, a slow smile crossed the queen's face, a smile so full of joy, so full of bright and absolute gladness that she could hardly speak. And when she did, it was in a low and halting whisper, and so she spoke through her tears of happiness. "So there is design after all. How strange, Lord Beryn, that you should be the one to teach me this." She shook her head slowly. "This time I will not yield."

Lord Beryn took a step toward us, then turned to Innes. "Boy," he said savagely, "I should have had you gutted, instead of holding you up by the ankles while the Grip did his work."

"You blinded this boy?" said the queen. "This boy?"

"How else was the secret to be kept, the king with his damn pale eyes?" From his pocket Lord Beryn took out a wrought gold ring and fitted it on his smallest finger. He held his hand out to look at it himself, then showed it to the queen. "I took this from around the boy's neck myself. Have you seen it before, Mistress Miller?"

The queen, with widened eyes, said nothing. The ring glittered in the morning's light.

"You did not know the boy was your son," said Lord Beryn suddenly. "You did not know."

But the queen smiled. "I did know," she said quietly. "The heart has no need of proof."

"Then know this too, Mistress Miller: Yield me this one, and I will let the other take the riddle's answer back to Wolverham."

"I will not."

He turned to me. "Boy, would you save the rebels or not?"

"The choice is not his," said the queen.

"Give him the answer and let him go," said Lord Beryn. And I knew then a terrible loneliness that I had never known before. To know truly that I was not the son, that was hard; to hear it spoken aloud, that was harder. To be sent away from her, that was hardest still. If the queen's hand had not been on my shoulder, I would have sunk with heavy loneliness. But she held me tightly.

"I will not let him go," she said to Lord Beryn. "I will

never let him go." She looked down at me, and the world was very still.

"This boy is nothing to you or to me," scorned Lord Beryn.

"Lord Beryn, he would not reach Wolverham alive with the riddle's answer," the queen answered.

A long moment passed. "No," agreed Lord Beryn finally, "he would not." He laughed suddenly and horribly. "You play the game well, Mistress Miller. Better than the king. He was right to send you from the castle."

"To send me from the Great Lords."

"Yes, to send you from the Great Lords."

The queen said nothing.

"As you will, then," he said, waving his hand as if to dismiss us. "There will be no answer taken back to Wolverham, the rebels will hang, and you three will never leave Saint Eynsham Abbey. Horses will sprout wings before any of you see the outside of these walls again."

"Then we'll be plucking horsehair from the clouds before long," I answered. Lord Beryn stared at me, then turned his back, crossed the courtyard, and crashed the door behind him.

I shivered in the breeze that he left, but the queen stood like a warm fire, gladness still on her face. Though we had failed in the riddle, and though we were prisoners forever in this abbey, her holding seemed enough just then.

When the sounds of shouted orders echoed into the courtyard, I pulled away and left the queen standing with Innes under the cherry trees, hand in hand. She looked at me, then turned again to Innes. I went back to Saint Anne's Chapel. I climbed into the loft to the deep, glassless windows and looked out over the common of Saint Eynsham.

A line of Lord Beryn's Guard sat motionless in their saddles, while behind them servants scurried about, beginning the encampment that would surround the abbey. The stark white tunics of the Guard menaced like an avalanche.

I stayed by that window as the day wearied itself into the afternoon, the sun slanting in a tight line across the far wall until it thinned to nothingness, and the loft darkening to shadow long before the day had ended.

I had known even before Lord Beryn arrived that the queen was not my mother. I had known it as soon as I saw Innes's face so close to her own. And there was in me a certain gladness for Innes. There was. But there had been that short moment in time when a place that had never known hunger before had filled. But now that it was empty again, a dull hunger remained.

A haunting hunger.

And it was Innes who came to try to fill it. Innes shuffling up the loft stairs, his fingertips gliding on the stone walls. It was Innes standing beside me near the window as the cooler air came in between us. It was Innes who knew how hot my silent tears felt on my cheeks. It was Innes who knew what it was that I longed for.

And it was Innes whose head cocked suddenly, and who shoved me back from the window just before an arrow sliced its way in, followed by a guffaw from one of Lord Beryn's Guard. I sat on the floor, breathing my heart out.

"We've already had enough bloody arrows," Innes said.

I stood up, panting, trying to keep some air in my chest. "I hear ... I hear that they don't hurt so very much," I said.

Innes swiped at me, and I took him by the elbow, and for a long time we stood still. "You are a prince," I said.

"A blind fool," he answered, and let me lead him down

from the loft and into the late golden light of the abbey.

Later the queen herself fixed our bedding in the outer room of her chambers. She sat, a blanket over her knees, and sang the same lullaby that the nurse had crooned to us in what seemed so long ago, until the melody sank into a soft humming. Then she snuffed out each of the candles, so the only light came from the reddening fire. The dark stole in slowly and comfortably. The song had lulled Innes into instant sleep, but I lay awake until she left, almost afraid to sleep, the dread of a dream I could not remember hard upon me.

And when I finally did sleep, the dream did rush in, only this time I knew whose arms were holding me: the queen's. But again the thickened air and the terrible light separated us, and when I thrashed about, I was still alone.

But this time the dream did not end there. This time there was another pair of arms, rough and jerky, that grabbed me and carried me upward into a cool and windy place. I was very, very high, and there was nothing beneath me but air, but that air was as solid and safe as living rock. I woke, sweaty but strangely peaceful.

The next day the Holy Sisters did not seem to realize that they were under siege. The routine of the abbey went on as if Lord Beryn's Guard were a universe away and all that mattered was that the old rituals be carried out, as they had been for who knew how long. The bells followed the hours with their ringing, the sisters chanted from the high tower of the abbey church and floated their prayers down upon us like soft snow. Every ritual was as it had been for day after day after day, as known and anticipated as the rising dawns.

"It is only to be expected," said the queen that evening in her rooms. The night had cooled with the clear sky, but in the small chambers the fire blazed the air and warmed the tapestries hung upon the walls. The flowers on them—brighter and stranger than any that even Da had fancied—seemed to swell in the heat, as if summer had suddenly come to their threads. "The Holy Sisters live more in the world of spirit than of flesh, and they can hardly be concerned with the politics of Wolverham when it is the politics of heaven that call to them."

"But they are besieged."

The queen took Innes's hand. She had held his hand, touched his shoulder, rumpled his hair all through the day, as if she had to feel him to keep proving to herself that he was there. "Perhaps the Holy Sisters know. Perhaps they do. But tomorrow morning will begin as it always has: with prayers, with silence, with the quiet matter of breakfast, with the gathering of water, with—"

"The gathering of water?" asked Innes.

"Each morning the sisters bring in the day's water."

"Where is the water gathered?" I asked.

And the queen answered with a broad smile.

We spent the rest of the evening planning the escape to Wolverham. The queen sent me with a message to the mother abbess, who directed the sisters to provide us with everything that we needed. Since we would not be able to take horses—Innes was the first one to point this out— we needed food for two days, warm clothes for the queen especially, and coins to perhaps smooth the way into Wolverham.

On the morning of our escape, I was awake when Innes sat up, clasped his arms around his knees, and turned his face to the east. "It's not quite dawn yet," I said.

"No. It will be in just a bit." I rose to build up the fire, and when I started the embers, they gave off their last fruity scents. Then I held still while Innes listened to the dawn. When he finished, we stood in front of the fire and put on the warm clothes the mother abbess had provided, then waited for the queen and for the routines of the abbey to lead the hours. We did not speak.

The bells rang for early prayers, and then again for the time of silence. From the queen's chambers we could see the morning rituals of Lord Beryn's Guard, who were interested in neither prayers nor silence. The night had been a frosty one, and they stood beating their arms against their sides, pushing in for places at the fire, shouting for the first hot food of the day. Their cries echoed against the quiet abbey walls and stirred their horses to nervousness.

All was so quiet within that we both startled when the door opened and the attendant brought in our own meal. "The queen fancied you might like—"

"Oatmeal." Innes grinned.

"—what with the journey you're about to take. And she said that it might be proper for me to be finding her own cloak about now."

"She has already set it aside." I pointed.

"Sister," said Innes, "we do not know your name."

She looked at him as if he had done her a great kindness. "Alyson," she said, and she spoke her name as if she had not said it for a long time.

"Then, Alyson, you will be careful while wearing the queen's cloak? You will stay out of the range of the arrows?"

Alyson leaned down and kissed Innes on top of his head, then blushed, half amazed at what she had done. She grabbed the queen's cloak and rushed to the door, turning back to look at us. The blush had not left her cheeks.

We ate the oatmeal—it was the same as the nurse had stirred, with cinnamon swirled into it—and drank the milk hot from the cows. "Innes," I said, "you realize that you are next in line to the king himself?"

He took a long drink. "Tousle, do you mind much?"

"That you will be king?"

"No." A long moment passed with no sound but the crackling of the fire.

"That the queen is your mother?"

"That she is not yours."

I set the bowl of oatmeal down. I had almost finished it anyway. "I was happier than I could have thought for those few minutes in the chapel," I said.

Innes nodded.

Then the door opened and the queen appeared. She was dressed in the long robe of a Holy Sister and held two more robes across her arm. "The attendant is walking along the abbey walls now," she said. "It is time for us to fetch the day's water."

chapter nine

Our robes must have been for Holy Sisters taller than us; they reached the ground and dragged over the frost. I held one end of a long pole, Innes the other, and we balanced it on our shoulders, careful to keep the buckets in the middle from sliding and knocking one of us in the head— and even more careful not to trip on the hems of our robes. The queen, her head low, walked just behind us. "You walk like two boys," she whispered. "You are Holy Sisters now. Keep your feet low to the ground, and your knees in, not out. Low, Tousle."

It was not an easy thing, to walk like a Holy Sister and balance a load of buckets, jerking our way across the commons and past the houses of Saint Eynsham.

"Keep the buckets balanced," whispered the queen again. "And your face down, Tousle."

"How can I keep my face down and the buckets balanced at the same time?"

"Lord Beryn's Guard is just ahead. Perhaps you might ask them," she replied.

Above us on the abbey walls, the attendant—Alyson—walked regally back and forth in the queen's cloak, as if taking the early-morning air. Beyond us the Guard stood grouped around their fires, watching the procession of twelve Holy Sisters come down to the brook. They quieted with our coming, and as we got nearer, I kept my face to the ground, even when I felt the bucket slide backward and clunk into Innes.

"The fresh morning of the world, sister." Lord Beryn.

The sister at the head of our procession said nothing.

"Sister," came Lord Beryn's voice, mocking, "shall we allow a mere siege to disturb the day? If I were as rude as you, I might forbid you this water."

"This water is befouled," the Holy Sister announced.

"Even the best of horses will do that, I'm afraid."

A snort from Innes behind me. A silencing whisper from the queen.

"We will go farther," said the sister, calling back to us. "Into the woods there."

"The greater the distance that you must carry the water," Lord Beryn pointed out.

We moved quietly upstream. I was sure to keep my knees in and my feet low to the ground. When there were only pine needles below me, I looked up and saw that we had come well into the trees, far enough that the three of us might successfully slip away, but not so far as to arouse suspicion.

"But," said the queen suddenly to the Holy Sisters, "they will see that there are only nine of you returning to the abbey."

"We will go back and forth in small groups. They will be easily confused."

I could have wished that the pine trees grew together more thickly, or that the lower branches had held on to more of their needles. A look behind us still showed the encampment. But when the queen motioned us ahead, Innes and I laid our buckets on the shore of the stream, folded our arms into the wide sleeves of our robes, and slowly, slowly, slowly moved upstream. It took everything in me not to break to a run.

If the cherry trees had been hopeful of the spring in Saint Eynsham Abbey, there was little reason for hope in the deeper woods. Most of the brook was still frozen over, the banks on either side iced with old snow. The ground was hard as gray slate, and the pine needles that springtime would soften were frozen upon it.

At first the queen led and we kept Innes between us, him holding on to the queen's long robe and sometimes to her hand. But as we moved farther into the woods, farther away from the Guard's encampment, we walked all together, never minding the branches that snapped off at our passing, never thinking that we should be careful about the trail. If the cold had not hovered so beneath the boughs, I could almost have believed we were on a lark, caring more about the going than the coming.

The queen knew that this stream flowed out from the river passing the old mill on the way to Wolverham. We did not ask how she knew this. We followed her because she was the queen, and because she knew the riddle's answer. And because she was Innes's mother.

And so we walked through the morning, a pale sky over us, a pale ground under us, following the stream in its windings, the heat of our walking filling our robes while the cold air tipped our noses.

Around noon the land began to jolt up around us. Soon we were in a small but deep valley, the pine trees clambering one atop another, up and up the steep sides. We stayed down below so we would not lose the stream, but it was a hard business. The snow was deep here, sometimes well above my waist, and though the top had crusted over, we broke through it with almost every step, so we left plates of icy snow behind us. Sometimes the snow lifted into drifts that hid the stream, and we had to blunder around them until we saw the black water running again. We were all as wet as if we had plunged in and out of the stream again and again, and I began to wonder how we would spend the night without the cold and the wet killing us.

For a time the queen broke through the new snow herself, but soon she left it to me to lead. I would heft a leg onto the top crust, push against it and hope that it would hold, then heft the other leg up. And once in ten steps I could stand on top for just a moment—until the next step. My crunching falls echoed against the steepness of the valley. We staggered to a frenzied exhaustion, feeling the frantic hours rush ahead of us as the sun started to yellow the pale sky.

Finally we decided to risk losing the brook and climbed up the valley sides. The snow was not nearly as deep here, but it was slick where the sun had melted patches that froze to ice in the night. All of us felt our feet slip wildly away and the calamity of a hip thumping on rock-hard ice.

"Perhaps," said Innes, picking himself up for the fourth time, "we should have tried the horses after all." We clambered back down the sides.

At the bottom we stopped to eat the bread and honey that the queen had prepared, though stopping let our sweat cool and chilled us even more. We ate quickly, ravenously, even the queen holding the bread with both hands and tearing at it. Then we ate apples whose insides had browned with the bruises that apples will suffer at the bottom of a barrel. They too had frozen in this wintry forest, and they tasted like icicles. I felt their cold nestle all the way down into my stomach, a cold like the black of a pit.

It was while eating the apples that we heard the sounds of horses high above us. The jangling of harnesses and rhythmic pounding of hooves struck down the steep sides to seek us out, and we stood in sudden and complete silence, Innes with his apple still to his mouth as the sounds above us grew louder and louder, then passed on and were finally lost. All that time we did not move, did not speak, did not look into one another's eyes.

"We are discovered," the queen whispered.

"Not discovered," said Innes. "Not yet. They know that we have escaped the abbey and that we must head back to Wolverham. But they have passed by."

"I wonder," said the queen slowly, "what our escape has cost the Holy Sisters."

We followed the valley, crouching now and listening for the sounds of horses. None came, and finally the steep sides flattened out and the trees thinned. Here the crust had melted and frozen enough to hold our weight. In some places it had melted enough to yield to hard ground, and we could walk on frosty land.

But the stream had gone. Sometime as we had clung to the valley sides, it had meandered away under the snowdrifts. The queen looked steadily at me, and I saw that she did not know the way to the river and on to Wolverham.

None of us spoke what we all knew: We would need to find a place for the night. The sky had thickened into a quilt of clouds, and the light was graying, blurring the shadows thrown on the snow into a general darkness. We were all hungry, but we did not stop to eat. There was simply the eternal marching ahead, me in the lead, Innes behind, then the queen.

And there was no doubt that she was the queen. All day we had tramped through the snow, with only a single break to eat. Her robe and skirts hung wet and heavy, the bottoms stiffened with frost. She had pushed back her hood, and her hair that had begun so tightly tied back had fanned out and flattened against her cheeks and forehead. Her breathing came loudly.

But there was no doubt that she would go on and on, that if she must, she would pick both of us up in her arms and carry us on her shoulders.

And there was equally no doubt that Innes would not let that happen, that he would go on and on.

And I too would go on. By Saint Jude, I too would go on.

But the world was running its course, and the coming darkness drew with it a wind that whipped us with its tail, pushing under and up our robes, lashing at us with a grinning ease. We had long ago lost any path, and we pushed and stumbled on now in hopes of finding a light or suddenly falling into a farmer's field.

But the trees were growing thicker and thicker again. Thicker and thicker, hunching together in a bristling line of pines. Soon they pressed so thickly on either side of us that there was only a single passage to follow between them.

A single passage! There was only a single passage opening between them! Not wide enough for one horse to pass another!

"Majesty," I called back. "Majesty, there will be shelter

ahead. A place to spend the night. And food. And hot cider."

"You'll have to pardon him," said Innes. "He also thinks that horses are gentle animals."

"You'll have to pardon Innes, who always thinks we're about to be lost."

"An arrow in the shoulder will do that."

"Oh, your eternal arrow," I scoffed. "Who was it who had to pull it out?"

"Who was it who couldn't help a turnip find its way out of a cart?"

"But," said the queen, and her voice was laughing, almost giggling, "there'll be no need for any pardons."

I looked ahead at the light that beamed through the woods, casting a long brightness down the path between the trees.

"I smell baking bread," said Innes.

"It will be a cottage," I said, "tidy and perfect."

And it was, of course. A cottage just like the one we had seen before. Everything was the same: the sharp roof, the cornices, the carved door, the twisting bricks of the chimney. Everything was the same, as if the cottage had not burned, but had lifted from its foundations and found its way here to this lonely spot. And when we walked in, the table was set with the same crockery, and the fire leapt up again to greet us merrily. There was the brown bread waiting on its warming bricks, and the jug of hot cider, and its steaming mixed with the steam coming up from our warming clothes.

We dropped our robes in a heap and stood by the fire so that it might melt the ice from our bootlaces. Then, with our feet held out to the flames, we sat and ate and drank and drank and ate, the heat of the fire thawing us with a delightful pain. The queen did not seem startled at the surprise of the cottage; she was not even startled to find three beds laid out in a loft. We never spoke of Da, but every time I looked around me, I expected to see him suddenly standing there, holding his pipe just out from his lips. For some reason I thought that the queen expected him as well.

Full and warm, we settled beneath plump covers that night. The jangling of Lord Beryn's horses seemed very far away, and I fell into a sleep with no dreams. I woke up only once, when I heard the familiar sound of a new log rolling to the grate and then arranging itself in the fire. The cottage was still as warm and merry as it had been when we had arrived, and I leaned down over the loft to watch the fire's brightness, thinking that Da might be down there tending to it. But he was not, and I fell back into sleep with a sigh, wondering where he was, wondering whether he would be standing with me when we finally reached Wolverham.

I was not surprised to find the oatmeal in the morning. Beside it stood a crock of milk, still warm, and the jug of cider, as full as when we had first come. We ate standing by the fire, as if we could fill ourselves with its heat and carry it with us. Outside, the sky showed thick and gray, and the few snowflakes that drifted out came from clouds plump with their downy filling. But inside, inside was everything that could be wanted on a stormy, cold day: food, fire, blankets. Da was so close here.

But there was only a single day to reach Wolverham, and we set off with sure steps, following the path given to us by the pine trees, watching the path push through the woods and shoulder the snow off to clear the way. Within an hour we had gone farther than we had all the previous day. And the queen! The cider had taken years from her, and she skipped like a young maid off to dance on the village common.

"You cannot know what it feels like to be away from the abbey," she called.

"Has it been such a prison for you?" Innes asked.

"An abbey is no place for a miller's daughter who once lived all her life in the fields and woods. Why, there were days when I was a girl that I would leave with the dawn and come back with the moon, climbing the very tallest pines or bending birches down and up again. There was a nob or hill—much like that one there—that I could climb straight up. Its rocks were just like those, and if you gripped there, and just there . . ." She paused, then tilted her head to one side and held back her hair. "It's the very nob," she said quietly. "The very nob. And that tree just beyond it—I've climbed it more times than I can count. You see, Tousle, that one branch broken off? You have to reach just above and . . . Oh!" She put her hands to her face as if she were suddenly startled by what she was seeing. "I'm home."

And grabbing both our hands, she bustled us through the woods—the trees stood well apart now—stopping now and again to exclaim at a place she recognized. "I built a lean-to here. You can still see the notches I cut." She ran her fingers into them wonderingly. "And there, where that one tree breaks into two trunks. Do you see the hollow? I would put apples and nuts in it for the squirrels, then stand there and watch them scramble."

On through the ever-widening woods we rushed, the queen almost glowing as her memories took on weight. Her laughter and her tears were all one thing.

"Majesty," I said, "the trees are growing fewer and fewer."

"Of course. We are just this side of a long meadow. And beyond that lies the road."

"But the trees give us less and less cover."

She suddenly stopped, breathless, then laughed and shook her head. "The past is such a temptation. I would have run headlong into it without realizing that the present is ever so much closer."

"I think," said Innes, "we would have run into more than that."

Then we heard it: the jangling and whinnying of a troop of horses. We knelt low to the ground and grouped behind the last of the pines. Beyond the meadow, rows of white tunics rode in pairs along the way to Wolverham. They moved very quickly.

"Oh," said the queen, her hand up to her mouth.

"They haven't seen us," I said.

"The mill . . . the mill is burned."

There was no mill to be seen. Some stones still held to each other, and a charred timber poked up sharply into the air. But that was all. The Grip had kept his promise.

"We cannot go there now. But the meadow?" I asked. "Who belongs to the meadow?"

The queen did not answer at first, and I heard her murmur a quiet prayer. Then she shook her head and pointed. "You see where the trees bend around to meet the road. The farmer's house lies on the far side of those trees."

"Then perhaps—"

"He would be of no help. He and my father argued once over the weight of his meal, and neither would ever forgive the other."

"Majesty, perhaps now we should try the farmer anyway."

She shook her head. "Millers and farmers can say fearful things to each other."

"Then," said Innes, "you will need to command him as his queen."

The queen looked at him, quietly and with love, and I felt my soul twist with the sorrow that Innes could not see it, and that it was not given to me. She put her hand along his face. "Then we had better go on. There is a farmer ahead who is about to entertain royalty unexpectedly."

But as it turned out, there was no need to command. Staying back in the shadows, we followed the line of trees around the meadow, and when we came behind the barn, there was the farmer loading bales of straw onto his cart, and on the cart itself, straightening the bales for their journey, was the miller.

We stood still in the forest, the queen with her hands to her face. Neither the miller nor the farmer saw us as we watched them in their companionable work, the bales hefted and stacked, hefted and stacked, with no words needed between the two and the work making its own heat. But there was no heat where we stood, and Innes stamped his feet and beat his arms against his sides.

Perhaps it was that movement that caught the miller's eye. He stared across the field, and when the next bale was thrown up to him, it hit him full in the chest and tumbled back to the ground.

"Your great clumpy miller's hands can't catch hold?" the farmer yelled up, but the miller was already tumbling down the cart himself. Then he was running across the field to us, running with the awkward gait of a man who has not run for many years. He stumbled in the furrows and caught at the air when he tipped forward, but he ran all the while. It was fortunate that the barn hid him from the road; Lord Beryn's Guard would never have missed his careening gait.

And so he came to us, and he grabbed the queen into his arms as roughly as he might have grabbed a sack of flour, the golden dust of the straw that covered his face catching onto hers. They held each other, and held each other, and all the while not a word spoken between them, and no need for one.

And then there was the miller's wife, the farmer not far behind her. And she with her hands up to her face too. Then the miller stood aside, the queen held out her arms, and the miller's wife was in them, pausing only a moment to touch the queen's face before she held her to herself, the scent of the straw strong around us, and a sudden sunbeam casting the dust of it to a golden halo around the three.

Then the queen turned to Innes, and the miller asked, his voice low and gruffed, "And is this him, then?" The queen nodded, and the miller picked Innes up in his two great clumpy miller's hands and held him to his chest, the tears coming suddenly and without pause. Innes reached to feel the contours of his face, and then the miller's wife took his hand and laid it onto her face, and the three of them laughed and wept together, the queen looking on until the miller drew her in. Then it was the farmer and I who watched that holy moment.

"Majesty," said the farmer finally, "the Guard are all about. They've searched the house and barn twice already this morning. And here we are almost in plain sight."

"The farmer is right," said the miller, setting Innes down. "And that"—he grinned—"is not something I say often."

"You should say it more often than you do, you donkey of a miller."

"You ox of a farmer, do something right and I will say it. Though"—and here the miller almost began to weep again—"he took us in, you know, took us in when our mill was still smoldering, as we stood with nothing left."

"And there's been no end of trouble ever since. Who would have imagined that a miller never learned to stack bales. Look at that cart. It won't make the road before it tips over, and then there will be the whole thing to do over again."

"Perhaps," said the queen, "it would do to—"

"Yes," said the ox of a farmer, "to get you all inside. And not all crossing at once so we don't attract unwelcome eyes."

"Let the eyes of the unjust be blind," I thought.

The farmer went first and slid open the barn door, then the miller's wife with the queen, the queen swinging her arms and striding as if her feet had never touched a marble floor. Then the miller and Innes, Innes walking confidently beside him, swinging his arms a bit too eagerly and tripping once, but no one from the road would have guessed that he was blind.

And so I stood alone. Absolutely alone.

Perhaps it was no accident that the sun faded at that moment, but with its going, loneliness fell over me like an avalanche, and I was startled by the hurt of it. I did not envy Innes. I did not. But the knowledge of how little I had froze me, and though I tried, I could not even drag up memories of Da, memories that might have carried a thaw with them.

So I stood alone.

And it was then that the mailed hand reached down across my face and stopped my mouth with its iron taste.

It jerked me up and back, farther into the woods, and in a moment I could no longer even see the barn, could no longer smell the pine and the straw—only the iron. Then my arm was whipped around my back and the voice of the King's Grip slithered into my ear.

"If you cry out, Lord Beryn's Guard will be upon us— and upon them—in less than a moment. And it will not be a queen and a prince they set their swords to, but a miller's daughter and her blind son. Do you understand, boy? Yell and you give the game away."

I nodded, still looking through the trees, straining to see the barn.

"They will go on without you, and who knows but that they might even reach Wolverham with their riddling. But they have no need of you now. And it's the last day, so they have no time to come back and search." He turned me around and shoved me forward, into the darker pines, where his black horse waited. There was no cantering away this time. The horse waited patiently while the Grip hefted me into the saddle like a bale of straw, then mounted behind me. He turned the horse's head and dug in his heels, and the horse spurted into the deeper shadows, back the way we had come. It had all taken only a moment. I wondered if they had yet even missed me in the barn.

"Your trail was plain as could be, even if Lord Beryn's Guard did not think to follow it. Boy, I could almost believe that you wanted to be followed. But perhaps you thought I had been killed?"

I said nothing. I ducked as branches swiped at us and tried not to think of the ache that was numbing the arm he still held.

"But I won't be killed. Not while I still have this search to finish. And I have waited for its finish for a long time, boy, a long time."

"I've searched for a riddle's answer to save a hanging," I said finally. "And what have you searched for?"

"He does speak! Boy, I thought you might have lost your tongue in all this. You should be thanking me now. If I had let you go on to Wolverham, it would be more than your tongue you'd be losing."

"If you ever truly served the king—"

"The king," the Grip snarled scornfully. "The king. As if he were a man I should serve. He fuddles about in his own fear, afraid to sneeze before the Great Lords give him the cloth to sneeze into. He armors himself like a god, then looks to Lord Beryn to see if he may piss that day. Do you think bringing the answer to a riddle will save a single life? Let the answer be what it may, Lord Beryn will shake his head and the hangings go on."

I knew it was true. Horribly, I knew it was true.

Farther and farther into the woods the horse took us, spurting forward with each dig of the Grip's heels. "You see there," he said, "those branches snapped at the trunk. Even without the snow, they would have given you away. And that spot there where one of you stumbled."

"Where are you taking me?"

"I thought that surely you of all people would know that."

And then I did know. He was taking me to Da's cottage.

"I burned the first one. At first I thought the logs were too weathered to catch, and then I thought there was some magic at work. But I piled up branches against the sides and set them alight, and the rest followed soon enough. It generally does. But now, to come upon this second one. Well, boy, that's evidence of design, wouldn't you say?" He laughed shortly, then spurred the horse again.

He never relaxed his hold on my arm, which was now numb and bloodless. But that was not what brought the tears to my eyes. I wished more than anything—more than anything—that Innes and the queen, and the miller and his wife, would come yelling down upon us. Sometimes I even turned my head to see if they were following. I knew that they had to reach Wolverham. I knew that they had to bring the answer to the king's riddle, even if they did not know it was meaningless. I knew that they could not come. But I wanted them to come anyway.

The trees grew thicker, and the horse slowed. The Grip had to lean down to follow our tracks in the thinner snow. But he was sure of the path, and soon I smelled the familiar smoke, and the trees gave way, and we were in the clearing beside the tiny cottage.

"He will come here, won't he, boy? Sooner or later the little man will come. And then I will trade you for the secret of spinning straw into gold." He released me and lowered me from the horse. Slowly I let the arm fall to my side, feeling the pain as the blood pushed back into the closed and stiffened vessels. I rubbed my hand up and down its searing muscles.

"It will come back soon enough." The Grip chuckled. "Now into the cottage. After this day I will never serve another man."

I pushed open the door and walked in. The bread and the cider were still by the hearth, warm and brown. I poured the cider into a mug and gulped at it, feeling its warmth come down into me. Only then did I realize that the Grip had said nothing since we entered. I looked at him. He was staring at the loft, staring like one who has found his heart's desire.

The loft was heaped high with straw, piles and piles of it,

fresh and golden, almost glowing, though the loft was in shadow. It spilled down in wisps to a spinning wheel, where a long strand had collected and twisted around the spindle. Beside the wheel, skeins of golden thread lay piled up, their round richness tumbling hugger-mugger all over the floor. It seemed that the wheel must have just stopped spinning.

None of this had been here when we had left. Da must have brought it. Da must have just been sitting at the wheel. If only he could come now and somehow carry me away.

Slowly the Grip crossed the room. He picked up a skein and stared at it, turning it around and around in his hand. He set it down, and pushed at the wheel, pulling his fingers back with the tingle of it. But the wheel spun around three times—*whirr, whirr, whirr*—and in that time it filled the spindle with half a skein of golden thread, drawing the straw from above. He pushed at it again, and the wheel spun— *whirr, whirr, whirr*—until the spindle was full. It dropped off the wheel, and another empty one leapt up from a basket to take its place.

The King's Grip lifted the skein, the light from it shining on his face. Then he set it on the mound of golden thread, tossed his mail gloves to the cottage floor, and clambered behind the wheel. He looked around and found the place for his foot, then pumped at the pedal. The wheel blurred to a whirl, and the empty spindles began to leap to the wheel, then fall off and pile up full around him. He stared at the whirling, his eyes glazing, his mouth pulled back to a grin. He kept pumping, and the wheel spun, and the straw twisted down from the loft, and the spindles fell with their full skeins.

Higher and higher the piles grew about him, now so high that he had to shove them aside with his knees. They spilled out over the floor, and the King's Grip laughed with the pleasure of it.

"Do you see, boy? I have the trick of it. I can spin straw into gold. Into gold!"

The straw kept coming and the wheel kept spinning, and no matter how much straw pulled down from the loft, the piles of it never grew smaller but seemed to plump up higher and higher.

I stood back from the whirling wheel. The skeins flew off in an arching blur, and the King's Grip had to push out with his arms to keep his wealth from overwhelming him. His eyes never left the spinning, and his feet never gave up their pumping.

And still the straw came down. And still the skeins piled up.

Suddenly the fire drew back into itself and with a sputter was gone. Yet the coiled gold glowed with a cold light all its own. I could only just see the Grip's face now, the piles had grown so high. He showed yellow in the glow of the gold, as if he himself had been turned into a spindle and the skein of golden thread was twirling around him. I stood against the door as the skeins tumbled down around my feet and covered the floor. I could no longer see the hearth, or the bread and cider that were perhaps still warm under all that cold metal.

"Stop," I called, "stop the wheel!" But he would not. He could not. If all the world had turned to fire and ice, he could not have left the wheel. His eyes followed the terrible whirling, and then the coils grew so high that I could no longer see the King's Grip at all.

I pushed the door open and backed out. The gleam of the gold spread and splashed against the trees. It turned even the black horse a cold yellow, and after a single whinny he stood absolutely still, his eyes fixed on the skeins that were now tumbling out of the house and into the clearing.

Slowly, slowly I walked to the horse, my hand up. I made no sound with my tongue this time as I unwrapped the reins from the branch that held them. Then I slowly came around, tested my weight against the stirrup, and mounted. "Now," I whispered, "that wasn't so very bad." I pressed my heels against his side and pushed forward.

But the horse did not move. I pressed again, harder this time, but he stood as still as if he were made of pine himself.

Then I knew. The horse would stand here, watching the tumbling skeins of gold. And the Grip's feet would pump at the wheel, turning an ever-growing pile of straw into an ever-growing pile of golden thread. Seasons would come and seasons would go, and they would still be there, forever spinning.

I leapt down and ran from that place as if it were cursed.

It was late afternoon, already the sun starting its slow fall. Innes and the queen would have wondered where I had gone, but the Grip was right: They had no time to search, and would be well on their way to Wolverham. But I kept to the path, now so well traveled that even I could find it easily. But I did not know what I would return to. The answer to the riddle would be gone, and no one waiting for me there. Perhaps the farmer would be willing to take in one more exile. And if he did not ...

Then there was the jangling of harnesses, and a loud and annoyed whinny. I stood still. It would be Lord Beryn's Guard. But I was nothing even to them now. The answer to the riddle was already on its way—and I was not the queen's son.

A parting of the sun set the light against the green boughs of pines, and the air softened around me. And I saw the horses—not the chargers of Lord Beryn's Guard, but two thick, broad farm horses, their great feet clopping and battering against the hard ground.

On one was the miller, his bow strung behind his back. On the other rode Innes. Innes, for all love!

"There!" cried the miller. "He's just there, boy. And he's escaped." He waved with all the fresh gladness of the world, while Innes jumped down.

I ran to them, clapping both hands on Innes's shoulders as he reached out to mine. "You haven't knocked him down with turnips, have you?" he asked, grinning, and his grin filled my eyes.

"Was that you, Innes, on a horse?"

He nodded. "They really are very gentle creatures, Tousle. You just need to be sure that you don't annoy them with clucking."

Now the miller too was down and beside me. "Are you alone out here, then?"

I looked up at him. This was Innes's grandfather—his grandfather. I had never known before what a grandfather could be. "All alone," I said.

He took a step forward, hesitated, then leaned down and picked me up easily. The sweet smell of straw still hung about him, and it mixed with the resin of the pines about us. He crushed me to his chest, then hefted me up and onto Innes's horse. "Not alone now," he said. He lifted Innes up and set him behind me.

And so we headed back out of the dark woods.

chapter ten

It was the farmer's idea that brought us to Wolverham.

"The way that clumpy miller stacked the cart, we would have to do it again anyway," he said.

"Those bales would make it to Wolverham and beyond," replied the miller.

The farmer said nothing. He walked to the cart, and as we watched from the barn door, he leaned against the bales. They came down all a-tumble, scattering about him. "To Wolverham and beyond," he mocked.

It was late dusk by the time he and the miller had stacked them again. "No, turn the bale the other way," the farmer insisted. "That one bale turned the other way. Yes."

The miller looked toward us with exasperated eyes.

While the miller finished, the farmer went to his cellar and came back with a small barrel on his shoulder. "Ale," he said, "for any thirsty guards at the gates of Wolverham." He carried it to the front of his cart, then beckoned. In the shadows we ran across the farmyard and crept into the square space between the bales he had left for us. "I'll set the ones above you myself," he said, winking, and soon he had closed off the darkening sky with them. The queen, Innes, and I sat quiet and dark, warm and cozy, surrounded by straw. We heard the jangling of the horses as they were harnessed, felt the tilt of the cart as the miller and farmer climbed on, then the first jerk, then another, and finally the rough rolling of the wheels that brought us onto the road.

I fell into sleep.

Almost instantly I was again in the stifling house. A glare of terrible light, and the choking air seemed to grow solid around me. It all came with a rush.

But this time I was not afraid. And even in the middle of the dream I was puzzled. There had been such terror before, and now there was none—none at all.

Then I knew why. This time I was not alone. Someone stood just behind me, someone with sure and close arms. With her breath she gave me breath, and her back shielded me from the heat and light. So we stood together in that room, until cool breezes lofted through and the light paled and paled until it was the light of the morning sun. And the cool breezes blew the walls down—they fell into a clattering of sparks—and we were alone together on a field whose green grass rose cool and sweet around us. If I had stayed asleep, I would be there yet—as sweet a dream as I could ever hope for.

But I woke to the jangling of harnesses and the hushed tenseness of fear. The queen reached out and put a hand to my shoulder.

The cart moved off to the side and jerked to a halt, and then the jangling horses passed us, the rumbling of their hooves coming up into the cart. We shook even with the straw packed around us, listening to rank after rank pass by, with never a break in the rhythm of the horses.

"There must be more than a hundred," I whispered.

"Many more," said Innes. "If only we had some wicked turnips."

I swatted him. "Perhaps," said the queen, her voice low, "you might prefer to stand up and wave your arms at them?"

We were quiet until we heard the last rider pass, and only when the cart scraped back up to the road did we relax again into the straw.

The road began to run smoother, then smoother still. Swaying back and forth with the rhythm of the pulling, we did not speak. There was an ease and pleasure in riding along so, knowing that there was nothing else to be done but the riding. I could almost forget that we carried the answer to the riddle.

Once more we pulled to the side of the road to let a troop of horses pass. Once more we held our breaths in the quiet of fear. And once more they moved by without troubling us, and the cart sidled back onto the road.

Then, just when it seemed that we had traveled much too long, the horses paused, hefted us up and over a bridge, and came down upon cobblestones. The straw muffled the loud rattle of the wheels, but we jolted back and forth now, and the straw fell in upon us, so we all three reached up to preserve the bales over our heads.

"The miller will be pleased to hear that even the farmer's baling did not survive the journey to Wolverham," I said.

"So he will," replied the queen, and she laughed low.

The stones yielded to rough planking, and a hollow echo marked our passing. Then the wagon stopped and one of the horses whinnied shrilly. A murmuring at the front, then laughter, more laughter, followed by a cheer. Then the cart jerked forward again, and so we came into Wolverham.

It was a coming different from a week ago. Da had said that what was spinning out then had taken its place on the wheel a long time ago, and I knew now that he was right. But was my beginning only a losing? I would bring the answer to the riddle, and Innes had found a mother. But what had I found? A larger world? A larger world only?

Or was it really larger at all?

As the cart crossed the market square, empty and quiet now, I felt the rolling wheel of the last seven days spinning around to the place where it had started. But for me, all its spinning had merely shed off scabs that I had not even known about, and I was all the bloodier for it. I swallowed hard against the lump that blossomed in my throat, and gasped at the pain of it.

The queen placed her hand against my cheek. "No need to fear, Tousle. No need." But she did not know what it was that I feared. I would have faced all of Lord Beryn's Guard with a turnip in each hand against all of their arrows, if only I could know with a fierce and unquenchable knowing that the day would not dissolve into wisps of chance, and that in the end I would not be alone.

The cart stopped, started again, stopped, started again, and finally stopped a last time. The voice of the miller came through the straw. "That ox of a farmer has finally found an alley dark enough to suit him." He climbed up and began to pull back the bales of straw. Almost I wished that they would stay a little longer.

But the queen stood, and I looked at her height, seeing her head dark against the now starlit sky, and I was comforted. It was thrilling to look at the queen and to know that at least for now, the patterns of the queen's life and my own—and that of Innes—had come together like chain mail. They were woven together, and one link could not be moved without the other. If only it would be the same after this day. Then Innes stood as well, and I, and the cold night air surrounded us and chilled us after the warmth of the straw. "Your Majesty," called the farmer, holding up his hand. And so we climbed down onto the streets of the city.

The farmer pulled out a folded cloak. "It may be that Lord Beryn will be looking for you," he said.

The queen took it and slipped the cloak over her shoulders. "Do I look like a miller's daughter heading to market?" she asked, smiling.

The farmer and miller laughed, but I stood silent. She did not look like a miller's daughter. She was a queen, and when she turned to me, she looked as a queen might look. She held out her arm and drew me in. "And now we shall see what provisions the good farmwife has sent. And afterward we will think about the dawn."

That night brought with it the first warm breezes of the early spring. They came up as if they had been massing just outside the kingdom's borders, and then rushed forward like a roiling cloud. They blew up and over the city gates, setting the icicles to melting, dropping soggy chunks of snow from battlements, and puffing gently into houses and stables, so that men and women and horses and dogs woke from sleep and sniffed at the new smells.

They blew against us as well, and at first I pulled my cloak tight against then, anticipating the cold. But the sudden warmth, the good earthy smells they carried, the unexpected spring pleasure, made me half forget why we were sitting on a cart in a darkened alley through the night. It set the miller whistling, and the queen suddenly held up the hem of her skirts and showed us the paces of a dance she had footed one festive May Day. She took Innes's hands in hers and brought him down from the cart.

"This foot forward," she said, tapping his left. "Now back, and then forward again. Then the other. Now repeat. No, the left foot first," and then she laughed as Innes shuffled back, then caught on with a sprightliness that only spring can bring.

"And now you, Tousle," said the queen, and I held her hands and danced to the farmer's whistle, and Innes clapped and danced, and then even the farmer took the queen's hand and, awkward and embarrassed, showed his paces. And when I looked at the miller, I could see even in the darkness the tears that hung at his eyes, and I knew why they were there.

So we danced and whistled through the night, until the dark sipped back the stars one by one and faded with its bloating.

The queen looked at the sky, then let go our hands and pulled her cloak more tightly around her. She thanked the farmer, who of a sudden knelt on both knees in that alley, knelt to this girl who had measured out grain in the mill across from his farm, knelt to the Majesty that she had become. And then the four of us left the alley to take our longest journey.

It was a crowded journey. All of Wolverham knew that this was the dawning when the riddle would be answered—if it was to be answered. It was easy to slide into the groups that huddled toward the castle. Everybody was quiet, strangely quiet, with never even a murmuring from one person to another. They walked like small mounds, cloaks pulled tightly around them and faces hidden, and I wondered why they had come to the castle. Were they coming to a hanging, or to a salvation? I wanted to shout out loud to stir them, but I was not sure that they would have lifted their faces.

As we came closer to the castle, its outlines grew stronger against the sky, which had already colored to a purple. We were pressed now on all sides by the crowds, and the queen held out her hands to Innes and me to hold us by her side. The miller stayed in front to shield the queen.

"Majesty," I whispered, "perhaps walking like a queen is not what you should be about just now."

She turned to me, then to Innes. "He would give me lessons in walking."

Innes smiled and whispered back, "He might teach you how to walk like a Holy Sister."

"No," laughed the queen quietly. "I do not think he could." She took a deep breath. "Now we shall see what comes with the day."

The way opened up into the courtyard, and the pressure of the mounds against us eased. For a moment we stood still, looking at the looming castle that seemed larger—though not grander—than I had seen it before. But it was not the castle that stiffened my spine. All around the courtyard, gallows had been erected in a grisly circling. Rough-hewn beams, still black in this light, stood wedged into the air, and from them hung nooses like coiling snakes. They swayed back and forth in the breezes, darker than the shadows around them.

In front of the courtyard Lord Beryn's Guard held themselves in a frozen circle around the prisoners. On the parapet above them the Great Lords stood in a curved line, completing the symmetry of the gallows. We pushed forward through the crowd, not daring to talk now, not daring to look at the gallows. It was as quiet as if there were not a single tongue in that place, as if everyone were holding back a breath to wait for what would come.

But as we pushed closer and closer, it was no longer so quiet. Now we could hear the clanking of the prisoners' chains and the weak coughs that came out. Innes leaned toward me. "Tousle, there were two young girls. Only about this high." He held out his hand. "Are they there?"

I stretched out my neck, but there were crowds between us and the prisoners, and it was still too dark. "Not that I can see," I answered.

Innes laid his hand on the queen's shoulder. "Closer," he urged.

The queen nodded and whispered to the miller. "Closer still."

He turned and looked at us, a half smile on his face. "Well," he said, "never fill a sack halfway." With a shrug of his shoulders, he pushed on.

The sky was a lighter purple now, and I could see Innes lifting his face to the sky, waiting for the bells of the dawn. But it was trumpets instead of bells that suddenly blared out across the courtyard, their notes iron cold and shrill. Then the line of the Great Lords opened like a gap-toothed smile, and the king strode forward, Lord Beryn half a step behind him at his right shoulder. The king was armored again all in gold, but Lord Beryn was somehow even more splendid. His armor was of a startling white, and in this half darkness it shone even more gloriously than the king's. At his side hung a scabbard, and it too was white. I imagined how cold it would be to the touch.

Together they stood at the edge of the parapet, and we were close enough now to see their faces. The king's was grim, his mouth in a straight line and his pale eyes looking over the crowds at his feet. Lord Beryn was smiling, though his eyes looked out to the gallows.

The king held out his hands and opened his mouth as if to speak, but then he hesitated. None of the souls in the courtyard had lifted their heads.

"People of Wolverham," he called.

Heads stayed down.

"People of Wolverham," he called again.

No motion. Not a single sound.

With a look of scorn, Lord Beryn came from behind him and raised his hands. "The dawn approaches, people of Wolverham. The dawn approaches when your judgment will be carried out."

Had it been only seven days ago when the crowds had cheered such words? But there was no cheering now. Only silence broken by the quiet coughing of the prisoners.

Lord Beryn tried again. "People of—"

But he was interrupted by a high, impossibly high screech of a young girl, a screech that resolved itself into a single word: "Innes!"

Innes broke from the queen, ran past the miller, and stretched out his arms to the cry. "Innes. Oh, Innes." A young girl, just so high, calling out from the prisoners, and Innes pushing through the crowd, his arms in front of him, desperately, desperately coming to her. "Innes, Innes," she sobbed over and over, stretching out her shackled hands. No one else moved in that great courtyard. No one else breathed. We all watched as the girl's cries brought Innes to her, until she was in his arms and he circled her. He circled her against all the power of the Great Lords.

"Eleanor?" he cried. "Eleanor?" And then a second girl, only a bit smaller than the first, threw herself at him.

Together they knelt, Innes laying their heads against his chest, the sobbing of all three mixing such joy and sorrow that it was a marvel the world could keep whole and not crack.

And now all the crowd had lifted and thrown back their hoods, and they stared at Innes and the two girls.

"You see, Lord Beryn, that you have lost your wager," said the king, who was now smiling. But he was not looking at Lord Beryn as he spoke. He was looking again into the crowd, searching—searching as if he had been filled with hope.

But Lord Beryn was no longer searching. With a motion of his hand he summoned up two of his Guard, and with a spurt they started toward Innes.

But they were not the only ones who spurted across the courtyard. With a battle cry of rage the miller was upon them. He grabbed their necks and threw the Guard back upon the stones of the courtyard. After that they did not move.

Another two of the Guard approached, but now the miller pulled up one of the fallen Guard's swords, and he stood in front of Innes, as menacing as madness.

"Not again!" he shouted. "By all that's holy, not again." He held the sword with two hands, high above his shoulders.

"Miller?" called the king wonderingly. "Is it the miller?"

The queen and I stepped forward, and now the two Guard turned to face us. But the queen pushed her hood back and held her hand high. "Move aside," she said simply, and the royalty of her voice pushed them back.

When I looked at the king again, there was a kind of desperate joy in his face. "The queen," he whispered, and his whisper was loud enough for everyone in that courtyard to hear.

"The queen indeed," replied Lord Beryn, "on a mission of such foolishness that I wonder she ever chose to undertake it."

"That you need to wonder, my lord, is evidence enough of your unworthiness," said the queen, and the words hung in the air like icicles that would not melt for any spring wind.

"Unworthiness, Mistress Miller, is not a word that you should speak. You have forced the king to the point of it. Let it be on your own head." He turned back to the king and waved at the crowds in the courtyard. "Your Majesty, renounce her now, before all your people. Renounce her, if you are to be the king you were born to be."

But the king did not take his eyes from her. "You came," he said, still wondering. "You came." He stepped from the parapet. She waited for him, standing with us by the prisoners. And all the while the sky lightened and lightened.

"The dawn!" Innes called. "Mother, the dawn!"

With a gasp the king looked at Innes, then back to the queen, then back to Innes. "What did you say, boy?"

Innes picked up Eleanor and held her in his arms. The other girl stood at his side, her hand in his, looking only at him. Innes did not answer the king.

"Lady," said the king.

But then Lord Beryn shoved beside him, the other Great Lords grouped just behind. "This is a peasant queen," he cried, "and no one in all of Wolverham will bow the knee to her. Not a one. Renounce her now."

And so the world held its breath once again in this courtyard, waiting for the king's word. Waiting, waiting, while

Innes lifted his face to the sky, and I knew that the dawn had begun.

The king moved forward again, past Lord Beryn, down the steps of the parapet, and held out his hands to the queen. "Lady," he said again quietly.

But she did not reach to him. Instead, she looked back at me, called me to her, and when I came, she took my hands and held them so firmly, so firmly, that I knew I would not be alone at the end of this day. "Tousle," she asked, "what fills a hand fuller than a skein of gold?"

And I knew this as well.

"Another hand," I said. "Another hand."

The queen drew my hands up to her lips and kissed them. Then she let them go and turned back to the king. She held her own hand out and took off the king's mailed glove; it fell to the stones, the gold of it gleaming dully at their feet. Then she slowly, slowly laid her own hand in his.

The joy that filled his face was no longer a desperate joy.

And the crowds were no longer quiet.

Such a cheering echoed in that place. The joy of those two touching hands spread until everyone in that courtyard was filled with it, and the walls echoed to the cheering, echoed to the calls and the laughter and the cries that carried in a blissful whirlwind up and up into the sky. And suddenly full dawn was upon us all, and light cascaded all in a white-water rush into the sky. And I saw Innes's face and knew he still heard more than the cheers.

But I could also hear Lord Beryn, who was not cheering. He too came down from the parapet and stood in front of the king with his back to the courtyard. "Do not challenge me on this," he menaced. "We will not bow the knee to a miller's daughter, or to her blind son. Do not challenge me. Renounce her even now and hang the rebels."

The king looked long into the eyes of the queen, and then, hand in hand, they both shoved past Lord Beryn and climbed back up the steps of the parapet. The king held his arms out over the crowd, and they quieted. "The riddle is answered," he called. "Tear down Lord Beryn's gallows."

Another cheer, and immediately the gallows started to sway drunkenly back and forth in the air. One by one they splintered and came down, each fall greeted with yet a louder, impossibly louder cheer.

And then as I watched, something lobbed from the crowd toward the Great Lords. It curved through the air, catching the new sunlight for a moment until it struck the chest of one of the Lords, who stepped back with a startled grunt. Another lob, and then another and another, and suddenly they were coming from everywhere in the courtyard, lob after lob battering the Great Lords, driving them back and back.

"Turnips!" I called. "Innes, they're throwing turnips at the Great Lords."

"Is their aim any better than—"

"Be careful I don't throw one at you!"

"If it's me you're aiming at, I'll be safe."

"So you would be." A pause. "Innes," I said quietly, "you came on a horse to find me. You came on a horse."

"I would have come on a rhinoceros."

At this I laid my hand on his shoulder—the shoulder of the next king.

But Lord Beryn was not finished. With a cry he grabbed a lance from one of his Guard and held it back over his shoulder. "There will never be a peasant king!" he screamed, and when the queen gasped, the king turned first to look at her, and then to where she was looking. Lord Beryn was pointing the lance at Innes.

"It is what I should have done when the brat was born. It is what I would have done had this miller's daughter not spirited the child away from me." He turned to the court-yard. "People of Wolverham, we will not have a peasant king!"

And with the words, he threw the lance at Innes, even as the king came leaping down at him with his sword out.

A cry from one of the girls. A call from the queen.

And I stepped in front of Innes. I held out both hands to catch the shaft, felt its wood slide eagerly past my palms, and then with a shock I jolted back. I was terribly cold.

And in an instant I was home with Da, him sitting by the fireplace holding his pipe. He sat back and puffed at it, watching me. He raised his eyebrows.

"No," Da said, "this is not his dream."

"Am I still ..."

"He is still alive. He is talking to me, after all." Da fussed with his pipe and tapped some of the ashes out onto the hearth. He filled it with a pinch of tobacco, then tapped it with his thumbnail to light it again. "It was I, he knows, who took the young prince from his mother's arms, never telling her that the king was too weak to protect his own son from the Great Lords. That he was too weak to protect even her. It was I who brought him to the village where he would be raised with another boy just his age. But I had left him only a few seasons before he was found out. His pale eyes could not be concealed, and word had spread."

"Da ..." I began, wonderingly.

He held his hand up. "No, I'll finish now, and then he may forgive me or not. When I returned to find the boy, the parents were murdered, the young prince gone who knows where, and only the other boy crying in the house that Lord Beryn's Guard had set afire. I thought the prince dead. And there was only Tousle left, all alone. So I took him myself."

"But you did not take me to another family."

"I did not. At first I kept him to spite chance, to teach it that it was not as powerful as it thought. But soon I kept him for another reason. And then I knew that nothing, nothing is ever quite by chance."

He came close to me and placed his hands in mine. "I came to love him," he said quietly.

I reached around him and held him to me, the sweet tobacco smell of him wafting around us.

Then he pushed back. "Almost I could not let him go to Wolverham."

"But when you found that the prince was alive . . ."

He nodded. "Then I knew that there was design, and if I would keep him apart from it, then how would that design finish its patterning? So to Wolverham, and the pattern of the young prince's life has woven itself together."

He was right. He was right. The pattern of Innes's life had woven itself together. But when his had been ripped apart, mine had ripped too. And where was my weaving? Where was mine?

"As for that," Da said, as if he could read my thoughts, "there is more for him to finish." Here he waited a moment, smiled, almost laughed. "And he has found his gift."

"My own gift?"

"A king's son can hear the dawn, a sexton can see in the dark, a funny little man with froggy eyes and spindly fingers can spin straw into gold. And his, his is the best of all."

"But what is it?"

The room glimmered, then began to fade. Soon all there was to see was Da, standing alone, still smiling. "He has the gift of giving himself," he said.

Suddenly there was a jerk and a stabbing pain in my shoulder, and I was no longer with Da. The warmth of smoke and the house vanished, and I felt the ice-cold cobblestones on my back. I wondered how it was that the stabbing heat of my shoulder did not melt them. I blinked and tried to raise myself up.

"Stay down," said the queen. "We have taken the lance out, but we have to stop the blood."

"Innes."

"I'm here." He was kneeling by me too.

"You know, of course . . ." I gasped as the queen began wrapping something around me. "You know that this is much worse than a tiny arrow in the shoulder."

He laughed, a laugh of relief. "You have beaten me squarely. Shall we say that this competition is over?"

Then it was the king at my side. "I shall lift you now, boy. No, miller, this is for me to do. If you put your arm about my neck, just so, yes, just like that . . ."

I gasped again as he lifted me. He stepped around something sprawled on the cobblestones, then carried me up onto the parapet. The queen and Innes came behind, and at the very top the king stopped and turned to the people of Wolverham. "This day," he cried, "this gladdest day of the world, this boy has brought back to me my queen and my son. This day . . ." and then he could not go on.

But he did not need to. As the four of us grouped on the parapet, the people of Wolverham cried out as if they had never cried out before, and they kept crying out long after we turned and went into the palace, long after we had come to the king's own rooms. I could hear them calling even as he laid me down gently, gently in a bed, and stood by while the queen tightened the bandage.

"The rooms have changed since I was last in them," she said quietly to the king, still tightening. "There is nothing gold about them."

He smiled and once more reached out his hand to take hers.

In the days that followed, the power of the Great Lords drained away in the heat of the spring sun. With Lord Beryn dead, struck down by the king's own hand, they scattered to the countryside. There was no one to rally them. They never recovered from their pelting, and wherever they appeared, people who had once feared them held wicked turnips high into the air. They had been made ridiculous, and people do not fear what is ridiculous.

First one, then all of them came back to Wolverham, where they bowed the knee to the king and queen, pledging their lands, their loyalty, their own selves. The king accepted that loyalty, and the queen lifted them from their knees and took their hands in hers.

It was an act of forgiveness worthy of a monarch.

The king and queen spent much time alone together, and they were often both bleared with the tears of many years. Together they rode through the streets of Wolverham and in the fields beyond, and often the queen would dismount, the king following, and she would introduce him to those she knew from her earlier life. Sometimes they rode as far as a small village on the way to Saint Eynsham, where they visited the sexton and the nurse in a cottage scented with herbs and bread—and love.

One day the king came home with his hands bleeding and scratched. He had helped to rebuild the mill that had been burned down and had spent the day learning the art of masonry. The queen herself wrapped them, and when he winced at the blisters and she clucked her tongue at him, he laughed.

It is no small thing for a monarch to learn to laugh at himself.

With Innes too they spent much time. The king set Innes in front of him upon his own horse. "He's quite gentle," the king said. And he was. They spoke little together at first; betrayal is not so easy to overcome. But as the king began to find the words to describe what he was seeing to his son, he began to see things for what they were and not for what they were worth. The wonder of it caught at his breath, and when his son took his hand, the king marveled that there had ever been a time when he had not known the answer to the riddle.

When Innes or the queen were not with the king, they sat by my bedside. I told the queen that I had seen Da in the delirium of the wound, but she did not think it was a delirium. She nodded her head at the story as if she had known it all along. "To believe that there is only chance," she said quietly, "I have known it. I had almost come to believe it myself." Then she looked at me, and it was all I could do not to envy Innes.

When Innes came from riding with the king, he almost always stood with his legs bowed out. "There is," he said, "much to grow accustomed to." He made me laugh until my wound pained, and when he found he could do that, he made me laugh all the harder. "It's something I can hardly help," he explained, holding his hands out. "And if it was me lying there, and you here . . ."

"Then I would do it to you," I said, and laughed all the harder.

Often he would come with the two young girls by his side. They were, he explained, orphans now just like himself . . . or like he had once been. They were shy at first and stood behind him, but soon they came to climb up on the bed and jump up and down and up and down, all the while the wound paining me. But I did not care; there was such a pleasure in them. And when the queen came and saw the hectic jumping, she held her hands over her mouth and laughed herself. "Does it bother, Tousle?" she asked.

"Never," I answered, and then I would throw a pillow at them, and the girls would squeal.

"He's throwing pillows at you, is he?" Innes asked. "Then you're as safe as safe can be."

And so the days went by, then the weeks, then the months, and it was high summer, where sunlight gilded the fields the livelong day. I was up now and working on the mill with Innes and his father. Our hands had grown as rough as the stones themselves, and at night our shoulders ached from the weight of the beams we had raised. But there was a pleasure to the good sweat of the work, and it told me that my shoulder was healed.

And one hot day we cheered the first turnings of the wheel. Then there was laughter and quiet talk. The miller's wife carried out trays of bread sweetened with golden honey—the king had never tasted it before—and we sat by the water and threw the crumbs to mallards.

Afterward the king and Innes rode into the woods, and I rode back to the castle, back to rooms that seemed suddenly lonely and still. For Innes the intricacies of his design had laced themselves into a whole. But for me, with my shoulder healed and the mill built, the next curl of the design was hidden. I would always have rooms here; the king and queen had smiled when they told me that, and Innes had looked puzzled, as if he could not have imagined anything else.

But my design was still not laced together.

One afternoon when Innes and the king returned from the woods, their heady calls came up even into my rooms, and when I looked out, Innes had just turned his face to cry up at me. "Tousle, Tousle," he called, "we've seen your da." He jumped down from his horse and patted her sides. "Tousle!" he called again.

I met him coming through the kitchen, where the queen was just bringing the last of her loaves out from the ovens. She sniffed the air that rose from them, and the warmth flushed her cheeks.

"We met the most curious little man, my dear," the king said.

"Tousle's da," said Innes. "It must be."

"So curious," repeated the king. "He walked out with the most curious gait from a tiny cottage and started dancing around a fire."

"And did he say anything?" I asked.

Innes shook his head. "Only a song.

'I brew my beer, I bake my loaves,
And soon my own dear son I'll see.
So Rumpelstiltskin bakes his loaves,
And soon my own dear son I'll see.'"

"Is there any more than that?"

"No," said Innes. "But if it was your da . . ."

"It was indeed," came Da's voice, and there he was. He sat close by the fireplace, his pipe just out of his mouth, and tried to hold back the smile that would creep up his cheeks.

"Da!" I cried, and then we were together, him a full head and more shorter than me. My throat closed and I could not speak. We stood there a long time, the smell of his pipe close around us, until finally he stepped back and turned his wet face to the queen.

"Mistress Queen, I never meant—"

"You meant to save my son," she said quietly; and with slow grace she curtsied to him, as noble in that kitchen as any queen might hope to be. "And now may I make my third guess?"

"You may, dear heart."

And the queen took her son's hands in hers and sang:

"I brew my beer, I bake my loaves,
And soon my own dear son I'll see.
So Rumpelstiltskin bakes his loaves,
And soon my own dear son I'll see."

With the gentlest smile, Da bowed to her, and she again to him.

Then the queen turned to me. "And is the design finished now, Tousle?"

"No, no, no," cried Da. "Not finished. Just one tiny part curled into itself." He turned back to me. "And now it is for him to decide the path of the next curl."

"The next curl?"

He held out open hands. "If it were not for me, his father and his mother, they would not have died. No, no, he must not deny it."

"I do not deny it." I looked at Innes, then back to Da. "I have forgiven it."

Da paused, then bowed once more, this time to me. "He has the whole world before him," he said quietly. "The whole world. He has only to step out into it."

The queen came and held my shoulders. "And you may always, always, step out into it with us," she said.

I looked ahead at the days as they placed themselves on the wheel and spun out their design. I knew that I would often be at the castle, and that I would stand by Innes one day when he himself would be crowned.

I knew that I would carry the queen's gentle touch on my shoulders always.

I knew that one day I would step out into the wide world. The design was so very open. So thrillingly open.

But the day to curl it again had not come yet. Not yet.

I filled Da's hand with mine, and he looked up into me.

"Da," I said, "are the Dapple and the Gray saddled?"

A long silence, and then such a cry of weeping joy as this old world has not heard in many a long year. Many, many a long year.

So we rode home together that day. When we passed the mill, the wheel was turning smartly; beyond, the wheat in the fields that we had seen barren so long ago was now close to harvest. The trees ahead bowed and parted as we reached them, and as we passed into the pines, they swayed back and forth.

They did not close again when we reached home. They stood open against the sky that the setting sun had washed to a quiet gold.

OAKLAND MEDIA CENTER